THE SON

A Conference of Victims
The Descent
The Great Petrowski
The Infinite Passion of Expectation
The Lights of Earth
The Mistress
Stolen Pleasures
The Tea Ceremony
Women in Their Beds

THE
Son

◆ A NOVEL ◆

Gina
Berriault

COUNTERPOINT
BERKELEY, CALIFORNIA

This is a work of fiction. All the characters, organizations, and events portrayed in this novel are either products of the author's imagination or are used fictitiously.

Library of Congress Cataloging-in-Publication Data
Names: Berriault, Gina, author.
Title: The son : a novel / Gina Berriault.
Description: Berkeley, California : Counterpoint, [2022]
Identifiers: LCCN 2022056976 | ISBN 9781640095977 (paperback) |
ISBN 9781640096035 (ebook)
Classification: LCC PS3552.E738 S6 2022 | DDC 813/.54—dc23/
eng/20221129
LC record available at https://lccn.loc.gov/2022056976

Cover design by Lexi Earle
Book design by Laura Berry

COUNTERPOINT
2560 Ninth Street, Suite 318
Berkeley, CA 94710
www.counterpointpress.com

Printed in the United States of America

1 3 5 7 9 10 8 6 4 2

My well loved and tender son, know and understand that your house is not here. This house wherein you are born is but a nest, an inn at which you have arrived, your entry into this world: here do you bud and flower. Your true house is another.

—AZTEC FRAGMENT
The Midwife to the Newborn

THE SON

I

On the night of the day she was graduated from a girls' school with twenty-three other girls in the same kind of virginal white gown, all floating under the trees with their ribboned diplomas in their hands, she demanded that her parents consent to her marriage to the brother of her father's mistress. The young man was nineteen, extraordinarily handsome and on his way to Hollywood where, with the help of a cousin who was an actress, he would become an actor. He had no money and no job other than as an occasional waiter in a big, cheap restaurant frequented by Italian families, and he could not act, so he could not, her father explained to her, ever hope for much to happen unless his beauty was so great that nothing more would be required, and this, her father said, was doubtful, for wasn't his head too large and his legs too thick, and wasn't he a bit pigeon-toed? Her father was an elegant man with a fine profile, and he made a practice, in times of stress, of deriding and condemning the enemy by referring to physical deficiencies. But swayed by his daughter's threats to accompany the young man anyway, and to bear a child to make matters worse, he consented to the marriage, and his wife consented also, and the wedding of Vivian Carpentier and Paul Cardoni took place in the Episcopal cathedral.

She had wanted as many guests as possible, for the greater the number the greater was the approval of her obsession with the groom, the more public the marriage the more assured was his future as an actor; that was the superstitious and substantive role the guests played. In Paul's old Ford they drove down the coast, stayed a few nights with the actress, then found a small apartment of their own; he went to work as a waiter in a famous restaurant patronized by the movie crowd and there awaited discovery. When she became pregnant, a month after the wedding, she looked forward to the child as a unifier of the parents. The child was to make the marriage last forever, though she had no doubt that it would anyway. But the pregnancy lasted longer than the marriage. Toward the end of the pregnancy he was troubled by insomnia, brought on, he revealed one night, by his dread of her bearing a child. The advent of a child unnerved him; he had not realized what a shock a child could be to the parents. He felt that his chance for fame was less now, he felt that he was chained to a rock. Since he revealed his feelings only one time, one night, she believed that he felt the way he described only once, as a person has a case of nausea one night and then no more. Not long after that night, however, he failed to return from his job, and nine days after his disappearance a letter came from Chicago, instructing her to return to her parents and to wait to hear from him. He was on his way to New York to try to get on the stage. He would, he wrote, send her an address when he got there, and he wanted her to let him know when the baby was born.

After riding all night on the train, she arrived just as her parents and her brother were sitting down to Sunday breakfast. She had not eaten supper the night before, having been revolted by the thought of food, and was hungry now; but hunger was not the only reason she ate with a gluttonous concentration. She felt that her parents had construed as wholly selfish her desire to marry the young man who had now deserted her, and, in their care again, she mockingly accepted their view of her by obligingly demonstrating the same kind of selfish desperation over the meal. She had been prepared for the world by her mother's celestial mauve ceilings and pale yellow satin sofas, yet here she was in her true nature: a girl with cheap, draggy pregnancy clothes given her by some neighbor's sister; her hair dried by peroxide and bleached two colors, white edged with sulphur yellow; her high heels turning under; her fingernails unclean; and too insensitive to lift her head for even a moment to say a gracious word to her family.

She sat in her mother's room while her mother spent an hour dressing and making up her face, apparently unaccepting of the reflection, patting her cheeks with rouge, twisting down hennaed curls to cover the cheeks. Vivian took cigarettes from her mother's porcelain box on the dresser and smoked them the way her husband smoked—after a long draw on the cigarette, throwing back her head to let the smoke trickle out. She crossed her knees, hooked her arm over the back of the chair, and swung her foot, while she told her mother about the actresses and actors into whose homes and pools Paul and she had been welcomed. She said that Paul had got a part in a movie that was being filmed in the Arizona desert, and she had told him before he left that she was going to visit her parents because he had been afraid she would be lonesome without him. At that point she broke into tears, sobbing so loudly she felt that she was wrenching the child out of place.

She lay limp and manageable in her mother's bed, babbling about cockroaches in the sink, grease-eating ants in the tub; blaming insects as the cause of her husband's departure because insects had been a constant irritant during a time she could not begin to examine, and because to examine the marriage, even if she could, was to see her life as she suspected her mother saw it, as a great prevalence of mistakes. Her mother covered her with a blanket, her and the large hump of her child, and went off to church.

Four days after her return, her father drove her late one night to the hospital, and the child was born in the early morning. She named the boy David, not in honor of any relative or friend but because the name had always appealed to her for its calling up of the youth who had slain the giant and in his manhood had become king, for the eternal youthfulness of it. The child had dark, downy hair and eyes like narrow luminous beads within plump lids, eyes of a deep yet indeterminable color; his feet were wrinkled and tinged with purple as if they were two hundred years old; and everything possessed that perfectness of miniature objects of art.

She was surprised by how her body responded to the child's cry when she herself was doubtful in response, unsure of how she felt about him—whether she would grieve if he were to be taken from her or whether she would be relieved, or whether she would both grieve and be relieved at once. When the child cried to be fed, a minute ferment started up in her breasts, an activity like that which might go on inside a fruit when the hot sun concentrates on it. The milk seeped through the cloth of the nightgown, and, when she lay on her side to feed him, the trembling draw of his mouth on her nipple tugged the womb upward in a most inward, upward pulling that made the sucking a pleasure for her and almost a reason for having borne the child. At these times she would caress his small, round head and his limbs of no angles, no joints, that had a curve like a doll's rubber legs, trying with her touch to perceive who he was, what manner of person he was to be, touching with a feeling of dread the hair that lay over the soft fontanel where the soul seemed to be contained. And even when, gazing down at his small face, she was disturbed by the inanity of his hunger, by the animal simplicity of his need to be fed and of his satisfaction while he fed, by this simple demand upon her because it forecast unknowable, more complicated demands, even as she felt in her spirit a shrinking away from his demands upon her and her future, her breasts responded to his mouth, her body enjoyed the secret and yet unsecret, the known to all upward pull within, and she was pleased with his dependency on her body.

Once, toward the end of her stay in the maternity ward, as she sat in the chair next to the bed, nursing him, it seemed to her a ludicrous mistake that a man should ever be in the condition of infancy. She wondered if he might be ashamed of her later—of the time of his infancy, and look at other male infants, even his son, and be ashamed for them. The time of his infancy seemed so absurd because there was already present in his person the time when he would be of significance beyond her—the girl who held him at her breasts, her two hands spanning his length. She was so amused by the absurdity of his infancy that she lifted him high to press her laughing face into the almost weightless combination of small dangling body and soft garments.

After one week she packed her few things, nightgowns and bathrobe and slippers. Her father carried her overnight case for her and she left the hospital, holding her baby wrapped in a blanket. She was careful of her step over the elevator threshold because she was wearing very high heels and taking some satisfaction in the fact that the shoes opposed the baby, that they hinted she was not in any girlish elation over the real baby in her arms, that the time of her delusion was over. In the walk along the corridor of the main floor and down the broad steps and out through the parking lot to her father's car, she fought an urge she knew she would never give in to and yet feared—to stumble in her heels and drop the baby. When her shoe turned a little, out by the car, she clutched the child closer in terror.

2
___

Almost every day, for the rest of that summer, she guided the canvas baby carriage down the hill to the park and sat on a bench in the sun and the moving shade of the trees, a girl in a pastel cotton dress, her legs and arms bare, her feet in sandals. There were always small children on the grass; and mothers, each with her disarray of kits and bottles; and there was sometimes a solitary man on a bench, a different man each time, who watched her over his newspaper or watched her without concealment. Joggling the carriage with her toe, she imagined herself with the man across the path, imagined a union so amorous that her husband would be wiped from her memory. Sometimes the proprietor of the grocery store gazed at her from under the awning, a small, green-smocked figure across the street, standing watchful. Was there about a girl with her first child, she wondered, the greater desirability of a woman who is innocently pledged? She speculated on her effect as she pushed the carriage home, pausing along under the awning to examine the fruit on the sidewalk stall, catching in the dimness within the store his gazing eye or the quick lift of his head.

The white, frilly bassinet was set up on its stiff legs and rollers in a corner of her room, and, when the child slept, she listened to the radio by her bed or read the novels that her mother bought, and the magazines, and was restless for the use of her body. The use of her body was enough; the rest of it—the belief that some-body else could know her spirit as well or better than she knew it herself—was a delusion. She lay on the bed, listening to popular songs or reading, with the fantasy of her next embrace always in the back of her mind, her body always waiting for the fantasy to claim it. She saw no ending to this time in her parents' home with her child other than the beginning of a time with another man, and in her mother's crooning and cluck-ing at the baby she sensed the wish for another man to come and take the daughter away. The wish was in the sweet, ardent, rather weary sounds as her mother bent over the basket, in the feminine ways of her body, ways exaggerated for the daughter to see and to imitate; since the daughter was now again at home and with a child, one must assume that she had not used and was not using her ultimate powers. As for her father, if Vivian were to run off with a man, he would not miss her, she knew. He lectured at medical schools on his specialty, the heart, saw his private patients, and spent almost every evening at his club or with his mistress;

his family had become like a group of patients he had treated when he had been specializing in a branch of medicine that no longer interested him but whom he was obliged to look over once in a while. Her brother, Charles, Jr., six years older than she and interning in a hospital across the bay, although he sometimes came home for a night, did not visit with her or show any interest in the child. When he did come into her room, it was usually in the few spare minutes before he left the house, and the contempt in his manner made her stand away from him and answer him grudgingly. She could not bear his loud, drawling voice, his calves bulging importantly against his trousers, and the long legs nervously shifting in professional style from one crepe sole to the other. When he asked her what she intended to do with her life, she told him, turning away from him, that she intended to take a course for charwomen.

She did, however, venture out, after a time. Her father's mistress, Paul's sister, was her good friend—a tall, almost harshly beautiful young woman, an advertising artist, who painted in oils and who had black walls in her apartment. Vivian often walked the two miles to Adele's to drink with her friends—newspaper reporters and commercial artists and actors. She sang for them one night, imitating a torch singer, perching herself on the arm of a chair, crossing her knees, languidly plucking at the drooping petals of a beige rose that Adele put into her hands. She sang again, a few nights later, for one of Adele's brothers-in-law, who owned a bar where the customers were entertained by singers and raconteurs at the piano. He had come over to Adele's apartment to hear her. She wore a dark brown silk dress that fit tightly and a long string of amber and jade beads, and her voice was insinuatingly low and warmed by the brandy.

The first night she sang in the bar, her parents came in together, hoping, she knew, that in spite of what they had learned about the lives of aspiring actors and entertainers, their daughter would be famous someday, bypassing the pitfalls. Her hair was cut short like a boy's, the shining paleness in startling contrast with her large, dark eyes; and her slender, young body affected the sensual indolence of the woman of experience, enticing yet seeming to remain aloof, waiting for the right one. The first few nights she was afraid that the patrons would suspect that she was fooling them. The gestures were not her own— she had learned them from singers in nightclubs and movies; the voice imitated that of an already famous singer, husky and plaintive with a controlled break in it; and the color of her hair was the color that was popular with movie starlets and salesgirls and carhops. As she repeated her act, it came to seem natural because the fixed, absorbed gaze of the audience and their applause led her to believe what they believed, that everything was natural with her, that everything was not a matter of trickery but of her own nature, as if she, herself, had originated all that was imitative and the others were imitating her. And when certain men in the audience became infatuated with her, this was further proof.

She became infatuated, in turn, with a big and amiable radio announcer, a widower in his fifties. He had a small gray mustache and gray curls brushed slickly back with silver brushes. She chose this man to make her body known to her again because he, among the others, seemed most affected by her. When he sat with her at a restaurant table, his fingers trembled touching her wrist and fingers, and his bass voice shook. He was not, she knew, the one who would mean more than her husband had meant, the one to rid her of the desire for others, but he was the one to break the link, her body's link, with her child. On the unmade bed in his half-empty apartment, he uncovered her breasts that had given up the mouth of the child only a month before and still felt the communion with the child; now the mouth of the man destroyed the link and, though it had to be destroyed, under the excitement she was disturbed by its breaking. Where the child had emerged, the doctor had sewn her into a virgin again, and the pain that resulted in the man's embrace seemed like an attempt of her body to repulse the stranger who was destroying the link with the child. She went up to his apartment often, and they lay in each other's arms for hours, approaching a tender respect for each other that took faults and failings into consideration; but always, when he rose from the bed and she lay watching him dress, his shirt tentlike around his hips, he became troubling to her and futureless.

No word had come from her husband since the letter written along the route of his escape, and at her parents' promptings she sued for divorce. The erotic atmosphere of the lounge was not, they implied, to be denied its possibilities. The child, at this time, receded from the center of her life. The Swedish cook and housekeeper, who lived in the servants' quarters off the kitchen, took the child to her room on the evenings that Vivian sang in the lounge, and her wages were increased for this extra service to the family. Sometimes, when Vivian had stayed out all night and slept all morning, she would go down in her robe, a sense of guilt upon her, and find the baby asleep in the bassinet in the sun filtering through the lace curtains in the woman's room, or gazing up at the canary in its cage. Although to sing and to be applauded was gratifying, and the nights with her lover exciting, she felt this was not enough to warrant her separation from the child. The separation seemed furtive, no matter how many accomplices she had. And she would make a show of love for the child, taking him up in her arms and carrying him through the house, laying him down on her bed or on a couch and nuzzling his belly and the soles of his feet; and the semblance of love passed over into the real.

3

With a grudging look of curiosity, her brother came into the lounge with a friend, a young resident doctor. She had met him, her brother told her, at her wedding, and she pretended to remember him. The young man, George Gustafsen, came in alone a few nights later and, talking with her, accidentally knocked his glass off the table.

He declared his undying love for her the first time he took her out and made the demand of her to love him as much. This declaration and demand were made while he sat apart from her in his car, then, without preparatory caressing, he threw himself upon her. She resisted him because his sudden ardor struck her as comic and because he was not pleasing to her physically—his face plump, his hips high and jutting; and he had the pomposity of her brother, as if he were emulating the other. After a few times with him, however, when he did not throw himself upon her but continued to declare his love and to demand that she marry him, she felt that his choosing her to be responsible for his happiness the rest of his life elevated her higher than anyone else had ever done, and she fell in love with him because of that oppressive honor and because a man so much in love, so possessive, so broodingly jealous, would surely take care of her forever and be true to her forever.

When she refused to go with the radio announcer to his apartment, he taunted her for her youth, predicting, with a pitiable meanness in his thick cheeks, her panic and loneliness at his age. She never saw him again. Even though she was sorry for him, some belief that no man was ever as helpless as he appeared to be, prevented her from feeling deeply about his condition. To think that a man was helpless was like thinking that the sun was helpless because it could not be other than a burning light.

The marriage to George Gustafsen took place in the home of her Aunt Belle, her mother's sister, in St. Francis Woods, the house strewn with red roses and a fashionable pastor officiating. The guests were relatives and close friends, but, reserved and small as the wedding was, Vivian felt that it was more than it ought to be, even as she had felt about the first wedding that it was not as much as it might have been. By this time she mocked all marriage ceremonies except the brief, civil kind, and made a practice of glancing derisively through the society section of the newspapers for nuptial items that told the fraternity of the groom, the sorority of the bride, the color and material of the bride's mother's gown, and for photographs of happy pairs, startled-eyed in all their trappings and suspicious of what the years were to bring in spite of blessings from God and pastors and parents and the bureau of licenses.

She gave up her singing in the lounge and sat at home evenings with her husband—the evenings he was not on duty—and with her son, who was at the time of her wedding almost two. She was again a wife, and although it was expected of her to be desirable to other men, she was to cease the overt demonstration, as in the lounge, of her desire for them. They bought a modest, two-story house in a neighborhood of narrow, stylish houses not far from her parents but not as commodious as the houses of her parents' neighborhood. She selected the decor with her mother, who was greeted by every manager in the six-story store, and in this decor, while David slept in his room upstairs and her husband read his medical journals and his *Time* and *Fortune* magazines, she sat curled up on the couch, knitting. She was acting, she felt, the role of a woman who has caused something important to happen to herself, and she was convinced that her husband was also acting; that his was the role of the young husband on his way to prominence and prosperity, content to be at home evenings with his wife, and proud that he was a loving father to another man's child. His legs were stuck straight out to the velvet

footstool as if ordered in that position by some director of the scene. It seemed to her that he was like a
boy imitating some perfect adult in everything he did
from paring his nails to lifting the child into the air,
from clearing his throat to predicting Hitler's next
move. She sympathized with him, for this need of his
to perform as others expected him to, but again, as
with her lover, as with Paul, her sympathy was baffled by the conviction that because he was a man he
was not in real need of sympathy, that he got along
very well without it, and that to grant it to him was to
take away some of his maleness—the more sympathy
granted him the more of his maleness was taken away,
and the less she thought of him. It was this troubling
conflict that led her one evening to sit on his lap, for to
be close against him, to be enveloped by his presence,
would rid her of her conflict, and she slipped onto
his lap with the innocence of a woman in the sway
of her own femininity, placing herself within his arm
that held the magazine and laying her head against his
chest.

She pretended to be as absorbed as he in the magazine, but the close-set type in narrow columns gave
her the same feeling of ignorance and insufficiency
that was given her by blueprints and the financial
sections of the newspapers. When he turned the page
and a picture of Mussolini appeared, of his big face
haranguing a crowd, she was instantly intrigued. She
touched the dictator's chin with her index finger and
the gesture was like taking a liberty with the man

himself, repulsing him and flirting with him at the same time.

"What's that for?" her husband inquired.

"Isn't that a monster of a chin?" she asked, afraid that he had guessed her trick of access into the lives of famous men. The only way she could get close enough to them to see that they were human was to imagine them making love.

"It isn't that bad," he said.

She waited for him to say something more and knew, unmoving in his lap, that there was to be some clash to enliven their evening and that both welcomed it and were tensed by it, and yet would have preferred to let the day go by without it.

"He excites you?" he asked, his voice as strained as if the Italian dictator were their next-door neighbor.

She felt a laugh readying itself in her chest at the comicalness of his jealousy, while her mind prepared itself for the seriousness of it. "I imagine he makes love like a bull," she said placatingly.

"You've imagined it?"

She shrugged. "Don't you imagine things?"

"There are other things to think about . . ."

"Oh, yes," she agreed.

"Let me ask you something," he said, and asked her then the question she knew he had been wanting to ask her ever since he met her. "Did you sleep with any man besides Paul?"

"No," she said, and laughed. "I was saving myself for you."

Their bodies became intolerant of each other and still she sat unmoving, hoping with the closeness of bodies to force that satisfaction in union for which they had married.

"You weren't saving yourself for anybody," he said.

She struck aside the magazine and got up. "You've been aching for me to confess ever since you met me," she cried, walking back and forth in her black satin mules, a hand on her hip, knowing how her buttocks moved in the black slacks, every movement substantiating what he suspected of her. Since their wedding she had felt a restriction on the grace of her body. He seemed, if she were graceful, if she were almost unconsciously provocative as she undressed, to suspect her of remembering someone else for whom she had learned those movements or of anticipating appreciation by someone other than he, and he would sometimes not touch her when she lay down beside him. But now in this promenading that preceded her confessing whatever little she had to confess, she recaptured her gracefulness, flaunting it because she had, for months now, suppressed it in fear of his displeasure and of his rebuff. She could not, however, confess her affair. It was the only thing she had to confess, but to confess it was to deny her right to it, to violate the secret matrix where knowledge about herself was forming like an embryo. She told him, instead, of the men she had been told about by the two dancers who had lived in the apartment below hers and Paul's in Los Angeles, but claiming those men as her own lovers. She told him the stories she had heard from the dancers who had talked endlessly of their lovers, enthralling her with not only each story but with the extraordinary powers they seemed to possess because of their profusion of men. If one man meant as much to them as to her, she had thought, what meaning there was in the profusion! And when the girls had laughed about each man's idiosyncrasies, she had wondered, and wondered now as she repeated their mockery, why they retaliated for that profusion of love. She threw herself into a chair, swinging her leg over its wide arm, to tell him in that sprawling position about her lovers, while he walked the room like a man mortally wounded and attempting to prove to himself that he was not. After a time he lay down and closed his eyes, but she knew that he still listened and would listen as long as she spoke.

She lay alone in their bed, her head filled with the surfeit of stories she had told, with the memory of her harsh voice claiming to know the frailties and prowess of men she had never seen, angry with him for imposing that surfeit upon her and the reluctant excitement of it. Almost everything she had ever done, it seemed to her now, was done at other persons' urging, whether they spoke their urging or did not speak it. The way she had walked around the room, and the way she flung herself across the chair, and the untrue confession, all were imposed by him. There did not seem to be any core within herself that was unaffected by him, by the men of her life, by her father and brother, by Paul and by her lover, and by her son.

At two in the morning she went down to shake him off the sofa. "When I didn't know you existed, why should I have waited for you?" she cried. "Why should I have waited even if I knew you existed? Can you tell me why?"—shouting down the opposing voice within her that said she ought to have waited because he had wanted her to, that all that was necessary was his wanting her to, even though he had not known her then, that his wanting was more than enough.

Upstairs, David began to wail. Unable to stop her trembling, she did not go up to him. Her husband, glad of the excuse to escape her, went up to the boy, closing the door after him.

She lay on her back, alone again in her bed, her hands clasped below her breasts, enticing sleep with that position, enticing with that innocent position a blamelessness for the use she had made of her womanness. That use of it as a weapon was not the use she wanted for it, and she was as dismayed by that use as she was by the entire eruption that followed upon her flirtatious finger on Mussolini's chin.

George wept dryly in her arms the first night he returned to their bed, after several nights on the couch in David's room, and she covered his head with kisses and confessed that she had lied and urged him not to weep, for she was unable to bear the sounds in his throat that were as unreasonable as their discord had been.

When the Japanese bombed the U.S. fleet in Hawaii, a change was brought about in their marriage.

Because they were now plunged into momentous times, swept into war and the unknown with the rest of the world, because of the imminence of separation or death, what it was that each feared in the other seemed not so fearsome, and they became inseparable. They seemed to have been mated by destiny—the condition that her husband had desired in the beginning.

In the blackouts they held hands, and, if David was still awake, they picked him up and held him and looked out the window at a dark city, imagining the suspense everybody must be feeling—the antiaircraft men and the sailors on the ships in the bay and the people at all their windows. She was aware of the thousands, the millions of people who held one another in the dark of other cities in Europe and Asia. She was aware of tremendous armies, of the magnitude of the seas and the land, and she was alive, as never before, to the near particulars of the earth—the tree in the street below and a solitary seagull soaring, its white breast made visible by the natural light in the sky.

George enlisted in the army medical corps and was flown East for training, and Vivian and her son were left alone. Before the child went to sleep, she told him about the heroic exploits his stepfather was to perform, rescuing wounded and dying soldiers, saving every life. But as she told her tales of heroism, lying on her bed with the child, her mind was not on the absent man but, with pleasurable fear, on the encroachments of the world on her life.

In that genteel neighborhood changes took place.

Late at night doors were slammed and voices were heard in the street, and sometimes she was wakened by curses and by footsteps running down the hill. She went for walks with David, who was three years old and ran ahead of her and off on tangents, up porch steps and into stores; she sat on a bench in the park while he played on the grass; they had lunch often at her mother's or at her aunt's or at her cousin Teresa's; she wrote every day to her husband and she read the newspapers; and her restlessness increased, the impatient waiting for the chaos around her to break in upon her. The country was in an uproar, millions of people were moving across the continent, whole families moving, armies moving from one coast to the other. She felt the vibrations of the city at work in the night; woke for a moment at midnight and knew that people were moving through the city on trolleys and in cars, going to and from the shipyards; heard the long convoys of brown, canvas-covered trucks rumbling through the streets in the hours before dawn; and knew, at dawn, that people were rising from their beds in rooms they had moved into the day before. It seemed to her that whole regions of people were moving into the city; she heard dialects that were like foreign languages, and strange intonations, strange pitches. Around her everything was in flux, and when she lay down beside David during the blackouts, the time of hiding in darkness with the rest of the people in the city was like a step into further mingling with them. She felt that she was using the child as ballast, as a mooring, and that, without him, if he did not exist, she might step out the door into the flood of change.

One night, before they fell asleep together, she kissed him over his face and head fervently, in need of protection from him, trying to kiss him into that condition of stability that she had desired from her husbands and that her kisses of adoration deluded her into believing they possessed. With her kissing of her son she wanted to persuade him to become at once a man and protect her from her desire to run out into the chaos. David whimpered against the fervency of her kisses, and she released him and lay back, turning her face to the window. The night was faintly illumined by the moon that was rising in that part of the sky not visible to her. She felt an exhaustion as after love and the dissatisfaction that at times combined with it, that desire for something more, as if something more had been promised her that was not yet given.

4

A friend of her mother's owned a dress shop off the lobby of one of the larger hotels, and she accepted a job there as a salesgirl. She wanted to sing again in a lounge, but that would be like an act of infidelity. Even her job at the hotel might seem like that to her husband, and when he returned for a few days before he was sent to England, she did not tell him that she was working.

The shop's windows faced the lobby and the street, both, and so the shop, with its gilded, high-domed ceiling, was like a display case for her. The hotel guests glanced in at her and she glanced out at them. She saw them as also on display, a passing display of generals and officers, industrialists, and diplomats. The hotel was like a hub for the entire war-frantic city. She saw them arriving and departing in immaculate uniforms and perfect suits, their faces not so preoccupied with their great tasks that she went unnoticed.

She sold dresses to wealthy women, some of them

her friends and her mother's friends, to discontented young women and young women delighted with their lives, and to elderly women whose sagging flesh was held up by elaborate corsets. Since her own mother was slender, Vivian had never seen women's bodies compressed and thrust up, and when these women took a long time to feel cloth between their fingers, or to decide for or against a ruffle or pleat, or to turn around and around again, in gowns and negligees, before the triple mirrors, their contemplation and deliberation seemed to her so futile. The war was not their concern; their anxiety was for their reflection in the long mirrors in the dressing room, whether they grew old like queens, as if age were an accretion of power, or sweetly, to placate the inevitable, or grew old retaliatively, as if everyone were cheating them of life. Among these elderly ones she felt a species apart, herself the only one of her kind, never to grow old and never to die.

In this gilded room with claret carpet and chairs of ocher velvet and rows of gowns on black velvet hangers, in this room fragrant with cologne sprayed into the air, where she was visible from the street and the lobby, she underwent a constant shifting of emotions. Her curiosity about the men who passed through the lobby or who came into the shop to buy gifts for women was chastened by her own need for fidelity, a yearning for her husband, and this shifting itself was exciting, a constant tremor of the heart.

She felt, at this time, estranged from her son. She

had hired a woman to take care of him, and the woman, Olga, lived with them—a spindly, aging woman with gray and orange hair and dark grape lipstick, who, because of an intolerance for racket, could not work in the shipyards, one among a few women, as she said of herself, not making a fortune sorting rivets and counting bolts. With no husband around who was generous with the child, as George had been, Vivian lacked the example. With no husband around to devote herself to, she had no desire to devote herself to anyone. She was with David only an hour or so in the morning and in the evening, and the impatience with him that had always been present now declared itself only as an uneasy deafness to his small, complaining voice and his screams of joy; since she was not so bound to him, she no longer felt so impatient with him.

She began to stay away evenings, serving as hostess at a U.S.O. center for soldiers and sailors. She enjoyed dancing with them, the change of bodies against hers, the many strange bodies responding to the strangeness of hers. Some of the men were appealing to her, the appeal of the few made stronger by the presence of the many. Teresa, her cousin, whose husband was also in England, took men home with her, but, for Vivian, taking a strange man to bed for one night was like taking a first step into that freedom which she preferred to titillate herself with rather than experience. Every day she wrote her letter or added to an unfinished letter. She wrote that she loved him, and she was sure that she did, but as she wrote her words of love, she imagined all the things he would condemn her for if she did them.

She was asked to supper one evening by her father's mistress, Adele, who had telephoned her at work, and, on entering the apartment, saw a young sailor stand up from the couch. The lamps, as usual, were dim, and in a moment's time she took a dislike to the laxness of his body, to the lazing pleasure the body took in its attractiveness. When he shifted weight, at her approach, from one foot to the other, an ungainliness in his legs, an overgrownness of his body, revealed him as Paul. Adele, sitting on the floor, her legs crossed, hugging an ankle with one hand and holding a wine glass with the other, jokingly introduced them as if they had never met, and they laughed with embarrassment, their laughter and voices sounding to Vivian like that of a couple who have always wanted to meet. Although, after he had left her, she had not known anyone who had meant as much to her, there was now no desire for him, only a superficial excitement. Adele served a feast despite the rationing, telling them it was done with mirrors and spices, and presided with a wide-gesturing charm that declared this young man her favorite brother and that denied she had ever ranted against him for his abandonment of his wife and child. He dawdled his fingers over the linen cloth, the arm of his chair, the silverware, as if his sense of touch had become more acute now that he was in the perceptive presence of two women who called for sensitivity; it was flattery done with gestures. He told them of his tribulations in New York; he had got a small part in a musical and found his legs rather heavy to dance around on; and with the closing of that show he had spent a year in Nassau as a companion for a very old and very wealthy man, but he had tired, he said, of reading his employer *Alice in Wonderland* every night, and then he laughed, apparently realizing Vivian was no longer naïve, that she might even have become more worldly than he and that his leaving her had contributed to her awakening.

David always came to her bed in the morning, while she reclined against the pillows and read the newspaper, and, with his legs under the covers, he ate his toast and sipped coffee and cream from her saucer and played with odd bits of broken jewelry and with a few small toys he carried in with him. Scrutinizing his features, the morning after her supper with Paul and Adele, she was pleased to find only a minimal resemblance to his father. She had known all along that the resemblance was only an undertone, but felt a desire to reassure herself about it. At four, his beauty combined the best features of her family. His hair, although resembling his father's in its thickness and its arcs of curls like the hair of Renaissance angels, was a darker brown, with a cast of amber red, like her mother's hair, a color she had always envied, for her own was the common light brown of her father's family and had always to be bleached.

David's eyes were blue, but darker than his father's, and there was a broadness across his eyes that Paul lacked, and a narrowing toward the chin. Under her scrutiny, he appeared to be more perfect than ever and more her own than ever, wholly her own and not the father's, who had inquired about him with his glance slipping away as if to inquire was to confess a crime. But, though he seemed more than ever her own, the elusiveness of his father, which had contrived to make the son her own, became the son's possession also. Although she nurtured him now and sustained him, his life was to be his own, even as his father and his stepfather appeared to belong to nobody but themselves, their lives their own though they were herded into regiments and battalions, into staffs and corps, onto transports, onto tremendous gray ships, and into battles.

When George was killed at St. Vith, she forgot his faults and remembered only his virtues. It seemed to her that his jealousy had indicated not a lack of understanding of her but a greater understanding than her own. He had prized her—that was the reason for his jealousy—and, prizing her, he must have known her essential self, the innocent self, and had struggled with her other self, the heedless, all-desirous self, as if it were his deadly enemy as well as hers. Nobody else would ever love her as much and understand her as well and join with her against the enemy within herself.

5

A few months after the news reached her of her husband's death, she went up, one evening, to the room of an air corps captain who had bought a lacy slip for his wife back in Boston. In the shop he had chatted with her about the two cities, comparing this point and that, and then had invited her to dinner. In a quick breath, nervously, he told her he had some Scotch in his room and asked her to come up before dinner so they could work up an appetite. Up in his room, after the Scotch had eased his nervousness, he was able to look at her for a long moment with his eyes unclouded by his fear of her personal life.

"You got a husband?" he asked her, like a doctor who has been told that psychologizing with the patient helps in the cure. He sat on the foot of the bed and she in the chair. "Ah, somewhere?" he asked.

She saw him glancing at her legs and wished that silk stockings were still available—the rayon kind weren't so flattering. "He's dead," she said, her mouth wanting the captain's mouth. She saw that his little blue eyes were surprised. "At St. Vith. He was a doctor, he was a captain with the second division. They gave him a silver star, he has a silver star," she said, tears slipping down her face.

"Ah, that's too bad," he said, alarmed, suddenly turning his head to see what was behind him. "You want to come over here and lie down?"

She lay on her back, weeping with her face exposed as if she had just received the news from this man. He lay down beside her, jolting the bed in an awkward attempt to lie down tenderly, and put his arm across her, and she wanted to relate every detail of her life to him because he had laid his arm across her comfortingly like a man who was to love her and protect her for the rest of her life. She turned her head at his prompting to enable him to wipe her face with the palm of his hand and his fingertips, and saw, above his fingers, the many intimate details of his face that was as close as her husband's had been, as the faces of the other men who had meant something to her, whom she had loved or had thought she loved; and she desired from that face, close beside hers, what all faces that lie close are called upon to give. She had imagined that, since his face was temporal, she would ask for nothing, only the time together, even the eventual indifference, only the transience itself, the excitement of the transient union; but now she called for the lastingness that ought to come from the one close on the bed. She gazed above his fingers into his eyes that avoided hers; at his sparse lashes that were here and there in clusters; at the coarse skin tinged with pink, a weatherworn skin with a few small scars so faint she knew they were childhood scars; at the flat, small ears and the very short, scrubby hair and the hairline where there were some few gray hairs, hardly different in color from the rest; at the thin lips concealing thought; and, having examined the minute particulars of his face, she kissed the palm of his hand as it crossed her mouth.

With his mouth on hers, he moved his hand over her body heavily as if receiving long, difficult messages through his palm. "Well, what pretty things," he said about her garments in the way. "What pretty little things," and helped her remove them with care while she kissed his hands and his body. "Well, what pretty things. You know you had such pretty things?" holding up her opalescent slip to follow its satin glow moving up and down the folds. "Ah, the pretty things to cover up the pretty things. One pretty thing deserves another, right? Never saw such pretty things in all my life. Look at that." Even if he had a wife in Boston, he might not be getting along with her, or before the war was over his wife might leave him, or the woman for whom he had bought the slip was not his wife. A man who could undress her with consoling words must be the man who would return to her.

But when he sat up on the side of the bed, rubbing his thighs, the bed moving up and down as he nervously rocked, the intent of the evening accomplished before the evening began and his gaze muddled, she

knew that he was to be for that time only. She drew
the blankets to her chin and lay grieving about his
temporality as if it were a surprise, a revelation, and
not a conviction that had accompanied her in the rising elevator. A sudden lowering of her spirits, an on-
slaught of reality, the elusiveness of the men she had
loved, Paul elusive by running away and George by
dying, all brought on a need for grieving under blankets. She watched this one as he walked around the
room, pouring Scotch—his bare, very muscular legs,
his short body and broad back, his bristle haircut and
small, flat face, his eyes narrowing to appear wise
when he came to the denouement of the story with
which he was bombastically entertaining her.

Afraid of other temporal lovers, she fell in love
with him to transform him into the lasting lover as
he hopped around the room, pulling on his trousers.

She clung to him in the taxi. She ran her lips up
and down his face and told him that there had never
been anyone so good to her, even her husband. She
would not release him when the taxi drew up at the
curb before her house and made him sit with her for
half an hour while she begged him to return to her.
The taxi driver, a woman, got out and took a stroll
down the middle of the street, her hands in her trouser pockets.

Alone in her room, she removed her clothes that
seemed soiled as though from several days of wear because she had already removed them twice that night,
once before supper and once again after, and felt a

rage take her over, a rage against the man who had left her at her door. She knew he would never write to her and never return to her, that he had rubbed his mouth against her face and promised to write only because the promising and the rubbing were part of the joke that he always seemed to be laughing at to himself and that he could not tell her, and she felt rage against herself for clinging to him, for exaggerating her wish beyond the true degree of it, when the truth was she wanted nothing to last, when she wanted to be as he was, elusive as he was. Wrapped in her negligee, she smoked one after another of the canteen cigarettes the captain had given her because so few were available to civilians, smoking them as though they were a glut on the market.

6

Her father escorted her one evening to a small lounge in one of the large hotels on Nob Hill. The manager sat down with them; he was a patient of her father's and deferential to him, ordering a cognac for them, chatting with them, and watching them put the glasses to their lips. Over in a corner a slight, blond man was pounding a baby grand piano, smiling over its dark, slanting wing at the men in uniform and their women, who crossed their knees when he sang at them, their short skirts slipping up their thighs. While she was glancing away at the couples in the dim light of the carriage lanterns, stirred by the crowding of bodies, the manager clasped her wrist and asked her to sing. He escorted her to the pianist, who seemed delighted, who said he remembered her, and she sang, picking up the tricks again, toying with her beads, coddling her voice in her throat, combining the skills of her voice and her body. She was hired to sing several nights a week, and she and her father drank together with the manager to celebrate. She knew that her father would be delighted by his daughter's becoming a famous singer as much as—or more than—he would be by his son's becoming a physician who was summoned to the bedsides of presidents. He was attracted to theatrical people, to artists, especially to bizarre artists of any field if they were elegantly bizarre, not imitative, not tawdry. He never missed a first night at the Opera House or a society ball, and even his everyday clothes had the touch of the actor—his dark gray form-fitted overcoat and his black homburg.

David liked to watch her prepare herself to go out and sing. He sat cross-legged on her bed with his head thrown back against the headboard, his mouth open because he was bemused by her and, since it was nine o'clock, half asleep. His eyes shifted from the glitter of the buckles on her shoes to the glow of the dress where it curved over the hips and the breasts to the fall and sway of the long string of beads. He did not often look at her face, he was used to her face and was, instead, intrigued by the animation of inanimate things. But sometimes she sang to him as she dressed, and he would watch her face then, as if it too were inanimate and the words and the tune made it flicker and change, as curious about the mechanism in her throat that made the low, strong whisper of a voice as he was about the central mystery of a performing toy; and while he gazed at the lively spirits in her garments and in her face, she was transfixed by him, in return—by the particulars of his beauty, the sturdy shape of his legs, his half-closed eyes and open lips, by the vitality evident even in repose. At this phase of his life, although all he could convey to her was what he perceived, as a five-year-old, of the workings of the world, she was more tolerant than she had ever been, more humoring, and more demonstrative of her love, because she was in touch with the world now, because she sang to those who were involved and who comprehended the world. All around the earth, armies battled and cities were bombed, and she sang to the salesmen and the manufacturers of everything necessary to the prosecution of the war; she sang to the generals and the admirals and all the uniforms of the services of the country in a hotel on a hill in a great port city.

She stood before the long, oval mirror, with imperious flicks of her fingers pressing the rubber ball in its golden net to spray cologne over her bare arms, watching her son, acting as an empress for him. Then she sprayed the air, high up toward the ceiling, pretending to wield an antiaircraft gun, and he laughed, still with his head back, his arched throat jumping. When she played with him during the day, he was often at odds with her, but in the evening, in this hour in which she felt no boredom because she was to leave him in a matter of minutes, she enjoyed the playing. During the day he was absorbed in his own self and she was his accomplice in that absorption, but now he became an accomplice in her self-absorption. When she pantomimed for him, acted silly for him, she felt that the audience later in the night was already gathered around her, enthralled by her entertaining her son.

"Olga!" she called, "did you make the bed?" And to him, "Never mind, we'll dump you in anyway." She held out her arms to him. "Come on, then. You want to fly into bed? You feel like a bird? If the war's still going on when you're eighteen, you can learn to fly. You can fly a plane."

He leaped into her arms, causing her to stagger in her high heels. With his arms clasping her neck, a leg on each side of her waist, and his face looking back over her shoulder, he was carried into his room.

"Up, up you go," she said, boosting him onto the dresser top. From there he jumped, arms outspread, onto his bed.

She threw back the covers, pushed and joked him under, and kissed him on the mouth when he was settled in. When he called to her while she was in her bedroom again, slipping her coat from the hanger, she called in turn to Olga to go and see what he wanted. With her coat slung over one shoulder, she passed his open door; Olga was sitting on the small chair, attempting a low, singsong voice that induced sleep. Vivian went down to the kitchen and stood drinking black coffee while she waited for the taxi horn, glancing at her dark red fingernails, turning her head to see the back of her knee just under the black dress, to see the high satin heel of her shoe.

7

The day that Roosevelt died she took her son for a walk to share the shock of the death with the people in the streets. She and her son went hand in hand along by the shops, and in every shop people were talking about the death, and the ones inside and the ones waiting to cross at corners all had a look of shock that—because it was not for anyone close, for father or brother or husband, for anyone they had spent a lifetime with, but for a great man—was touched or tainted with a sense of privilege: that they were granted a time beyond the life of the great man was like a sign of favor. The sorrow that she felt over the President's death became an encompassing sorrow for the millions of others dying, the anonymous others dying, and her husband dying, and for everything that went on that was tragic and that was not known to her. But as little as she knew, she thought, her son's knowledge was only a fraction of her own. He was not even aware of nations and their governments, of the

year and the era, and much less of the irretrievability
of the dead; but if he did not have the comprehension
now, he would have it in a few years. In a few years he
would have more than she had at this moment, a great
man himself, perhaps, about whose death—when he
was seventy or eighty, and she was already dead a long
time—everybody would be informed by newspaper
and by radio. They walked slowly because that pace
was suited to the day of mourning and to her son's
small legs; yet, after a time, the slowness began to an-
noy her. There seemed to be too much imposed upon
her in that slowness, the dependent age of the child
and the tremendous death of one great man.

In the evening, among the patrons of the lounge—
among the men who, although they were subdued by
the death, were nevertheless bathed and shaved and
manicured and brilliantined and brushed and polished, and anticipative of pleasures that night with the
women beside them or women waiting somewhere
else—she gave herself up to the exciting paradox of the
living opulently mourning the dead, and something
more came into her consciousness of the magnitude
of the world. At night in the bar with the changing
patrons, the changing faces in the dimness moving in
and out of her vision with more fluidity, more grace,
because of the solemnity of the night, she realized,
more than earlier with her son, the extent of a great
man's effect upon the world, the extent of the power
he seemed to have even after his death, the extent of
power over death that all these men seemed to have.

She sang the president's favorite song, and the pianist played it over and over again, pounding it out like a dirge while the solemn drinking went on at the tables.

Her father came in with Adele and with the actress who was to have helped Paul into the movies, a woman small and delicate, with a broad, flat-boned, powdered face, her shoulders emerging tense and arrogant from her ample fur coat. With her was the actor Max Laurie, a tragic comedian, always in each of his movies in love with the hero's woman. A civilian at the table next to them, whose shoulder was near to Max's, leaned over between him and the actress, gazing with a pretense of idolatry from one to the other, amusing his two companions, two men, with his intrusion into the glamorous company.

"It's a sad day," he said to Max. "You agree with me it's a sad day?"

"We agree," said the actress.

The man turned his head to look at the actress appealingly, a flicker of ridicule crossing his face. "Anybody who disagrees is a dog," he said.

"Nobody disagrees," said the actress.

"You ever met him?" the man asked. "They say he liked the company of actors and actresses. Banquets and entertainments, he liked that. Like a king, you can say, with his jesters. I thought you might have met him."

"Never did," she said, turning her back on him, drawing up her fur coat that lay over her chair so that the high collar barred his face. Then she turned abruptly back, as she would have on the screen, while the man's face was still surprised by the fur collar. "Are you envious because you won't die great?" she asked him.

"I'm living great, that's all I want," he said, and his companions laughed. "If you want to know another fact of life, because you don't know all of them, it's this: If you're living great, the odds are you'll die great. Like in the arms of some beautiful woman, right smack in her boodwah." And while his companions laughed, he looked around at Max and at Vivian and at her father, and since they were not regarding him with annoyance, he looked again, boldly, into the face of the actress.

"He was a wonderful man," said Max, his rich voice conciliatory, simple. "I met him myself. A bunch of us were out making speeches for him, can't remember if it was his first term or his twelfth." He had a way of lowering his eyes when everybody laughed and glancing up with a smile that suspected, shyly, that he was lovable.

"What was your name?" the man asked.

"Max Laurie," he said.

"Is that Jewish or is it Scotch?" the man asked and everybody at both tables laughed. "He loved everybody, didn't he?" he went on, striking their table with his palm. "Regardless of race, color, or creed. He had no discrimination—is that the word?" and overcome by his joke he bowed back over his own table, in silent tussle with his laughter.

Vivian left the table to sing again, and when she returned, the actress had moved to the chair Vivian had vacated, and she sat down in the actress's chair, nearer now to the intrusive man, and saw that he was observing her, his face that of an outsider, desirous, recriminative. "I guess he thought he was going to live forever," he said to her. "You could tell he thought so by the way he smoked that cigarette in the longest holder I ever saw outside of the movie queens back in the flapper days."

"You saw his picture when he was at Yalta?" she asked him, repeating an observation she had heard earlier. "He looked sick then, his face looked as if it got the message he was going to die. He had a blanket or an overcoat around his shoulders."

He patted her wrist. "You're sweet," he said.

"How do you know?"

"Because you got nursey eyes. 'He looked sick at Yalta.' Did you hear that?" he asked his companions, who were no longer listening to him. "You got nursey eyes." He took her hand between both of his, caressing it between his palms, attributing to her, with that pressure of his hands, a sympathetic knowledge of all men. "Go on."

"Go on what?" she asked.

"Tell me some more."

"More of what?"

"Oh, they got so much on their minds they don't take care of themselves. More of that. You know when a man gets a lot on his mind what happens to his body? Look at Gandhi—that's what's the matter with me. I'm as skinny as Gandhi only more because I'm twice as tall as he is. I think big thoughts. My head is big, see, but all my hair has turned white and my body is skinny."

"What big thoughts?" she asked him.

"We all got a stake in it," he said. "Those who stayed at home as much as those who laid down their lives. Got two factories going day and night, one down in El Segundo, out near the beach where the aircraft factories are. We make a small part that you girls would call an itsy-bitsy part, but without it the plane couldn't fly. It couldn't fly. Got another factory up here, feeds the shipyards with another itsy-bitsy part. When the general goes marching through the surf up to his neck, we're right along with him, you and me. You and me, we're right there when he delivers the coop de grace. The coop de grace belongs to you and me."

He brought their clasped hands into her lap and, opening her hand, he began to smooth it flat, palm up, insistently smoothing out her fingers that curled again after his hand passed over them.

8

On the night when the lights of the city came on again, she walked several miles before she hailed a taxi, elated by the glitter and glow of the signs, by the suffusion of colors, by the colors pulsing through the tubes, crackling and humming; by the animation of the signs whose borders ran in a demented pursuit of themselves, or each letter of the letter before it; and by the lights reflected on dark windows and gliding along the windows of passing cars. She saw the change of colors upon her white coat and upon her legs as she walked and knew that her face was tinted with the colors that she walked through as were the faces of other strollers, and this coming on again of every light was like an absolving of everyone in the city and like a mindless promise of further experiences that might call for further absolving.

The Manufacturer—she called him that, amusing herself with the anonymity of it—appeared again in the lounge. He brought no friends with him and he spoke to no other patrons. Their first night, when everyone had left her alone with him, she had gone up to his room and she had been delightedly aroused. Yet, after, she had wanted to seem uncaring if he were not to return, she had wanted to seem as elusive as she expected him to be, and with that she had brought him back to her. When they lay together again, his hands caressing her seemed to be discovering her for the first time, not having truly known her that other time.

He stayed four days in the city and promised to return in two weeks. Now that the war was over, he said, he would be in the city more often, conferring with his brother-in-law who was an investment banker. She no longer called him, jokingly, the Manufacturer. His name was Leland Talley, and she bought him six fine handkerchiefs with his initials in blue silk thread, and read her intimate knowledge of him in those fancy letters that could be felt under her thumb.

When he returned in two weeks and telephoned her from the hotel, she asked him to come to the house. It was early afternoon and David was home from school. He stood up from the floor, where a number of his toys were set about in some inviolable scheme, and shook hands with the visitor. Talley's manner with the boy was brusque and affable, his eyes veering away, distracted by other things; he seemed to resist being charmed by the boy's beauty, as though to be charmed by it was a sign of weakness on his part and the boy's also. David engaged in a fervent telling of an involved and unfollowable tale, his voice high and nervous and monotonous, his face without expression as he talked on and on intrusively, as if he had gone deaf and could not hear her and her visitor talking between themselves, as if he saw their mouths moving without voices.

Up in her room she dressed to go out to supper with her lover, who sat on the bed, his drink in his hand, watching her every move—the lifting of her arms for the slip to slide down, her hips within the slip as she walked to the chair, and the extending of her leg as she drew on the stocking with a graceful working of her fingers. Whenever she glanced at him as she talked, he narrowed his eyes, as if caught at some speculation that she was not a party to. Was he thinking that a serious affair with her might break up his marriage? She resented his hardheaded thinking about it, and yet was pleased that his resistance to her was falling away in her presence.

While she was brushing her hair and he sat watching her lifted arms and the pale curls springing back from the brush, David slipped in through the half-open door and, speaking at once, bowing his head over a toy he carried, he walked directly to the man on the bed. Something was wrong with the toy, he said, some wheel, some part was lost or stolen. "Right here, right here," he said, his voice high and hypnotized, "here, here. It's a clock. The lost wheel pushed the blue wheel. It was a red wheel but it got lost. The hands don't go. The big one—it was yellow—fell off and this one is loose, the little one, the green one. The wheel is gone on the other side. Right here, you see? The red wheel is gone." His complaining voice was a high, driving chant that, possibly, could endure to the end of the night. She called to him, but he failed to hear her. She called his name again, but he would not look at her or come to her. Instead, he sat down on the floor, his head still bowed over the clock. "Right here, right here, it used to be a big yellow hand. It used to go around when you wound it here. You could make it any time you wanted, you could make it any time of day." He went with them down the stairs and to the front door, the clock left behind on her rug, warning them about the dog next door, instructing them as to what they were to do if the dog attacked them.

After that day, the appearance of her lover, every few weeks, did not result in her son's acceptance of the man. Instead, David avoided him, apparently ashamed of his behavior that first time, or not ashamed but brooding over some other way of appeal. He kept apart from them and was not inquired after by her lover, who brought a gift for him occasionally but left it lying on the sofa or on a table. And in the early months of her desperate love for the man, she could not, she knew, be tolerant of her son's intrusion if he were driven to intrude. In the time between her lover's visits she was consumed by her longing for the man. She thought of him incessantly, and on his visits underwent a complete abandon at the first touch of his hand. She lay in his hotel room for hours while he went out into the city to attend to his appointments, waiting for him to return to the bed and to her body.

She no longer sang in the hotel lounge because the time there sometimes interfered with his visits. The months—almost without her consciousness of them, because the present was a combining of longing and fulfillment—ran on through the first year, and each last day and last night of his visits were always for her the peak of that combining. It was understood, at the beginning, that his wife was ailing and that he could not, now, approach her about a divorce, and that, since his factories were in a state of upheaval with the end of the war and his plans were to move with his wife to San Francisco and to become a partner in his brother-in-law's investment firm, for a time their love must await the stabilizing of the other factors in his life. Over supper tables and in his hotel room or her bedroom, he talked a great deal about his factories, about conversion. There were complications in his reports that were unsolvable for her, and yet she felt that he was not really attempting to establish the truth, the reality, for her, because he thought it too much for her to comprehend, that he was not telling her much of anything, only the skimming, only the jokes repeated by the clerical help, only the froth that rose from the turbulence of the business, from the heavy maneuvering. But this was enough, it was all she wanted to know, the rest was his domain.

With the diminishing of the intensity of their

times together, in the second year, some certainty of the future had to compensate for the lessening. When he and his wife moved up to Hillsborough, a few miles from the city, his constant proximity, then, was a substitute for that certainty, was an approach to it. And yet, as the months went by, that proximity of both himself and his wife in a colonial-style home upon several acres of landscaped grounds served to make the certainty grow more distant.

He was as aware as she of the slow abating, but he was not apprehensive of the end; he did not appear to believe that the end was approaching simply because the zenith was passed. He was now involved with his brother-in-law in plans for investment in Japan and the Philippines, and something of his optimism was transmitted to their affair.

"Listen, there's going to be big things in Japan," he told her. "Got to start their exports going, got to help them rebuild. I'm going over and take a look around. You want to fly over with me?"

The invitation to go with him to Japan was an intimation of something more, a return to the zenith, even a promise that she was to be his wife; it served for several months as proof of the constancy of their love. Then he left without her, promising to take her along the next time, explaining that this time was to be for a minimum of days.

She drove him to the airport, and as they stood together in the corridor he said to her, to the crown of her head as she was fingering the buttons of his overcoat, "You know why we're crazy about each other? It's because we're apart so much. If we go on like this, it'll go down in history, won't it? With those great passions? If we lived together, some of that crazy wildness might get lost, and I don't want to lose a fraction of it. We've got something I don't think anybody else ever had."

She looked down at him crossing the ground to the plane, ready to wave should he look up at her in the window of the waiting room. He seemed a man designated to bring about a prosperous future for all concerned, and his stride appeared so quick and purposeful she wondered if he might always be worried about missteps. The morning wind was flapping his trouser legs and lifting his white hair in tufts. He bent his head to enter the plane, a habitual bowing in doorways that were high enough.

When he disappeared into the plane, she was seized by fear, convinced the plane was to fall from the sky, plunging into the ocean. Out in the parking lot, trapped in the roar of planes flying in low and planes rising and vanishing into the high fog, she asked herself if she would want him to die rather than leave her willfully. Then she wondered how much she loved him or if she loved him at all, if such a question could cross her mind. Dismayed by her own mind, she wandered the parking lot, lost, unable to recognize her own car.

9

On the way to her room, at midnight, she entered her son's room. The window was up a few inches and a cold wind was stirring the curtains. Out on the bay the foghorns were sounding, expectantly repetitive, like a deep-spoken word. She sat on the edge of his bed, shivering in her negligee, watching him, his face plump with sleep, his arms flung above his head. If now, at the end of the affair, she doubted that she had loved, if her life was spent in seeking and pleasing some man, if her life was spent in need of his need of her, was love nothing but desperation passing for love? Was the only love that was not a delusion her love for her son?

The confusion, the terror she had experienced out at the airport returned and she began to weep, wanting to waken him with her weeping, wanting him to come up out of sleep to a consciousness of her. She lay down on his bed, facing him, facing his small, awake, alarmed face. After a time, realizing, perhaps, that her weeping was not caused by him, was not his fault, he began to stroke her hair and her cheek. Her love for him was not a delusion. He was the person in whom reality was posited; he was abiding, he was constant. Since the room was cold and she was lying on top of the blankets, he threw the top quilt over her, smoothing it around her so that it formed a cocoon, and she slept that way for a time.

Olga had left them, returning to Idaho some months before, and Vivian, rising early in the morning, went down to prepare breakfast for her son. After she had called him several times, he came down, still in his pajamas, and she saw his sullen resistance to her, a stubborn contesting with her, as if too much had been exacted of him the night before. He sat at breakfast with his eyes down, and when she asked him if he were going to school in his pajamas, he told her he was not going that day. When she tried to tug him upstairs to dress, he went limp, and, unable to drag him, she left him there, a small figure in blue and white striped pajamas, lying on the stairs. He remained all day in his room in his pajamas, coming down for his meals and going up again and closing his door.

The following morning she forced him out of bed by pulling down the covers and dressing him herself. He ate his breakfast and permitted her to slip his yellow raincoat over his back and over his limp arms and jerk the hood of it over his head. In the moment before she thrust him out the front door, she saw his small face, smaller within the yellow hood and paler in the gray light of outdoors, gaze out with a failing of his resistance to her, enthralled for that moment by the mingling of fog and rain, by the change of weather. The first rain of fall made the streets and sidewalks dark and glistening, and the leaves of the slender trees in their wire enclosures by the curb were moved erratically by the drops. She thrust him out, and he sat down on the steps. At ten o'clock, looking out the round glass in the door, she saw him still on the top step, throwing pebbles from the potted plant. The drifting rain, slow and unabating, glistened on his yellow raincoat and hood from a long accumulation. The small, stubborn figure forecast a future of contesting: they were to be alone together, and whatever was to trouble her would be for him only a reason for contesting. She called him in from the neighborhood's sight and, when the door was closed, turned him to face up the stairs and struck him across the back. With no retaliation, no anger, he went up the stairs, and the paradox of the fragility of his very young body and the power of his will led her to strike him again across his back.

The next day he got ready for school, ate his breakfast, and left, all with the casualness of a habit that had not been broken. Some time in the days that followed, before Leland's return from Japan, the conflict that had gone on between herself and her son roused her to an awareness, more than ever before, of the boy's separateness. He was someone unknown. And she acknowledged the pleasure for her in that unknownness. She took pleasure in his strong will. In those days of her lover's absence, she grew fascinated with her son's beauty, with the slender shape of his bare feet, with the thick, dark hair with its cast of amber red, with the hard blue of his eyes, with all the particulars of his face, the pliability of his lips. He had grown shy about his body without her realizing it. When the shyness had begun she could not recall, but her awareness of it now led her to become less concealing of her own self. With only a negligee around her she drank her coffee at the table while he ate his breakfast, the translucent, ruffled garment falling away from her breasts; with the door to her room open, she undressed or drew on her stockings while she sat in her slip; and she returned from her bath to her room with the negligee clinging to her body.

On the day of her lover's return from Japan, he telephoned at midnight, speaking to her with a teasing, insinuative voice, and in another twenty minutes he was there, roving his voice, which he seemed to have realized on his trip might be a means of arousing a woman, over her neck and down over her breasts within the white negligee she had bought a few days before. They went up the stairs together, his hand moving over her back under the negligee. In her room, her lover sat down on the velvet bench, drawing her to stand between his knees as if she were attempting to escape him, delighting her with that vise. She put her hands on his head to brace herself against the languor that was pulling her down, against his unbalancing of her as he moved his knee between hers to open her thighs.

She closed her eyes, sensing that her son was in the doorway and must be driven out, and, opening them again, saw him there, his small figure in pajamas, gone before her lover could turn to see what had caused her to push him away. She hid her face, clotted with shame and anger, cursing her son for intruding upon the heart of her privacy, yet knowing that neither shame nor anger was as strong as she was making it appear. With a twist of the brass knob she locked the door and lay down on her bed, stricken silent by the commotion within her.

Leland, still on the bench, untied his shoes, laughing softly. When he came down beside her, there was a remainder of laughter in his mouth and in his teasing body, and not until after their loving did she ask, "Why did you laugh?" But he was already asleep and she already knew the answer. He had laughed because the years with her were to lead to nowhere, and so he could make light of her son's curiosity and even use it to their advantage.

With the end of the affair, the false anger she had felt against her son became true. She was angry with him because he had always baffled her conscience, and she recalled, often, the shock of his small figure in pajamas, there in her doorway. She avoided him and he avoided her; he went to school, did all that was asked of him, and avoided her, besides.

One morning, when she had not heard from her lover for several weeks, wanting to impress upon him her remorse for asking for certitude when no one's future gratification was ever certain, she telephoned him at his office and was told by his secretary that he had gone to Japan again. She locked herself in her room and wept as if someone else had locked her in. She walked the room, smoking and weeping. A woman alone was obviously a sinner, had obviously not done something right or done all things wrong, and the aloneness was inflicted upon her to bring her to a comprehension of the enormity of her sin. She longed to be forgiven by her son for the time she had struck him across the back, for if he forgave her for that, then it would serve as a forgiving of more, of all her sins, those she knew about and those she did not. He had seen her in her worst moments and in her best, and, though he was a child, she felt he sensed who she was more than any other person sensed or cared to sense. Nobody else knew her so well. Nobody else was so near, so near he could walk into the heart of her privacy, knowing that her anger could never make him less a son, less than the dearest one.

IO

Up in the hills above the Russian River, her father owned a farm inherited from a bachelor uncle who had grown apples and raised sheep. He went there in the winter, taking a few friends, to hunt deer and quail. Nothing was grown with purpose anymore. The trees went on blossoming, the apples went on ripening, and there was a small grazing flock of sheep, a few chickens, a few pigeons. Everything was watched over in its cycles by an elderly woman who had been a painter in the city and who preferred the solitude on the farm, wearing old jodhpurs and hiking boots, her hair peppery gray and cut as short as a man's.

In the late fall of David's ninth year, her father suggested that she bring her son to the farm on the same weekend that he was there with a few friends; he would take the boy hunting and teach him how to handle a gun. She drove up with David a day before her father and his friends were to arrive, and in the evening they strolled out into the orchard. The sheep, wandering in the fields and under the apple trees, trotted up to them. Several were afflicted with colds and made burbling noises as they breathed, and out in the twilight and the cold she felt a sympathy for them as for neglected children. Down below, a long drift of white fog, touched by the daylight still in the sky and by the moon rising, was moving along above the river, fog more silent than the fogs on the bay that came in filled with sound, the deep and high sounds of horns on the bridges and the ships. The call of the quail was fading into the night, into the bushes and groves of trees. Strolling out with David, their sweater collars turned up against the cold, against the darkness sifting down over the low hills around them, she longed to feel in communion with him. The distance was still between them. After school he stayed away, doing whatever it was that boys together kept secret from their parents and that gave him a wordless wildness, an aura, at night, of the entire day of boys and secrecy, his face like the face of a leader recalling treason or of a follower recalling humiliation. On this stroll with him in the orchard, he told her nothing of himself, though the possibility for closeness was there in the beauty all around, the silver fog below, and the rising moon.

While David slept way up in the attic, she sat with the woman in the parlor. The wood-burning stove sent out its waves of heat, and the large parrot hung upside down in his cage and hid behind the tasseled shade of a standing lamp, curling his claws and tongue in a cawing, clucking, moronically cunning flirtation. The woman was knitting a red sweater; under the yarn her thighs were heavy in the faded jodhpurs. She had been gregarious in the city, a ponderous raconteur over cheap wine, a good friend of Adele's; but in the four years up here on the farm she had become a hermit. For an hour Vivian leafed through several magazines, chatting with the woman about their friends in the city, and, going up early, she felt that the woman was not offended and even preferred to be left alone.

She went up the narrow stairs that were lit by the globe in the hallway on the second floor. The door to her room was open and the lamp on, and she could see the bed covered with a reddish quilt, and the dresser with a long white cloth, and on the cloth a hand mirror with a tarnished silver back. Reluctant to enter her room, she climbed the staircase to the upper reaches of the house to look in at her son. He might be regretting his choice of sleeping quarters and willing to accept a small bedroom of his own on the second floor. Climbing the staircase that was enclosed by age-darkened walls and lit with a dim globe for the convenience of her son, a globe that would not be lit the other nights when the woman was alone, she was afraid for herself, a fear that, someday, she, too, would be able to be alone, like the woman alone in this house.

The top floor was not partitioned, as below, with bedrooms. It was one large room under a peaked roof that came down to the row of casement windows at each side, and, on one side, under the windows, were three cots. In the middle cot she saw the small, dark hump David's body made under the olive-drab blankets. From up here, the fog along the river was seen in its dimensions; from the window it had a breadth and a depth that seethed with moonlight. Way down in the yard and out in the woods and the orchard, the silence appeared to be the moonlight, to be tangible. She crossed the bare floor to the other side of the room and leaned on the sill to look out the open window, but a low hill, its top at a level with her eyes, seemed to crowd against the house, an obstacle to the view she had expected, and the trickery of the scene increased her fear. She went down again to the parlor, hearing on the way down the woman talking to the parrot. She explained to the woman that it was difficult for her to sleep in a strange house, and she sat down on the sofa, leafing through the same magazines and chatting again until eleven o'clock, when they parted.

With her father came two friends, the actor Max Laurie and a man younger than both, whom she had not met before. The three men in winter jackets and boots got out of her father's gray Chrysler and began to cross the yard to the house. The men turned when she and David, on higher ground up in the orchard, called to them. In a row, they watched her and her son approach, and the memory of her fear, the night before, was dispelled. The farmhouse and the cold orchard and the yard in which they waited for

her—everything was filled with the presence of the
men as with a clap of thunder or a flooding of hot sun.
When they began to turn away, because it was a long
way for her to approach, and to look around the yard
and lift up their faces toward the hills and the water
tower, she took her son's hand and ran with him, and
the running passed for a welcome from a woman un-
aware of herself in her happiness at seeing them. She
threw her arms around her father and around Max
and shook hands with the young man who, up close,
was not so young, was in his late thirties, the coarse
skin of his face incongruous with the young stance of
his body as he had watched her approach.

She walked with him to the house, while David
walked ahead of them between his grandfather and
Max, and the presence of the men was the reason for
her presence on the farm. She admired her father's
build, his erect back and his elegant head; and admired
the small figure of her son in the pearl-gray sweater
her mother had knit for him, his straight legs in jeans;
and admired the self-conscious sprightliness in the
actor's body. They brought her—the three men—the
excitement of pleasing them, the pleasure of pleasing
them. She was glad that none of them had brought a
woman. She was the only woman. The old woman in
her hiking boots did not count as a woman; she was a
past woman.

They had drinks together in the parlor. David
drank hot cocoa and sat by Max, with whom he ex-
changed riddles and jokes and she, the only woman,

listened to her father and Russell talk about the nightclub they were to finance in partnership with a shipping-company executive, and, engaged with them, she felt the riches of her womanness—in her gestures, in the ease of her laughing, in the appreciation in her eyes and in her body of all they told to interest her and amuse her. And she saw that the man who was new among them, Russell Maddux, was glancing at her with that alternating peculiar to some men, a desire for her and a concealing of desire that passed over his eyes like a curtain shutting off their depths.

They all went out into the woods early in the afternoon to hunt quail. She and her son were each given a shotgun, Russell instructing her in the use of hers and her father instructing David, and in a line they went through the brush and among the trees. Russell was to her left and Max beyond him, and to her right David and then her father. For the first time David had a gun in his hands, and she saw that he strove for an ease in his walk, an experienced hunter's grace, but was stiff in the knees and the elbows. The space that was between her and him; his face, glimpsed in profile, set forward timorously, transfixed by the quail that might rise up in the next moment; the awkwardness and the grace of his small, slender body; the blindness of his feet in sneakers—all roused in her a desire for him to remain as he was, the only one and the closest one, the dearest, incontestably more dear than any man who was to become her lover and who was now a stranger. While she was bound over to the lover, her son might leave her forever. Walking three yards away from him—walking gracefully because the man to her left was a few feet behind her for a moment and was perhaps noting the movement of her buttocks in the tight, trim slacks—she felt a strong desire to embrace her son and to beg him not to allow another man to lessen her closeness with him, not to allow her to give herself over to another lover.

A covey of quail whirred up, skimming over bushes, flying over the tops of the low trees. One was brought down, her father assuring David that, although both had shot at the birds, he had missed but David had not. David began a babbling prediction of hundreds of more quail brought down, and had to be cautioned by her father to be quiet. After that first shot, David's attack on quail and cottontail rabbits was almost ridiculously pompous, more confident than the men's.

They tramped back through the cold woods—in the bag four quail and two rabbits among them all—and on the large round oak table in the kitchen tossed the game down. She was standing across the table from her son and saw his face was flushed from the cold, his eyes narrowed by the intense excitement of the day, and it seemed to her that the span of years between him and the others, the men, had disappeared.

They stayed late around the table after a supper of roast lamb, of fruit preserves—the figs and plums of the hot summer—drinking brandies and smoking, talking about the division of Germany, and Russell about his experiences in the war in Europe, and Max about his entertaining the troops. David stayed with them in the parlor until midnight, listening and recalling at every chance everything about the hunt as if they had not accompanied him and were eager to hear, and when at last he fell asleep on the parlor rug, she roused him and went up with him. He fell onto his cot, too weary to undress, and she pulled off his shoes and waked him enough to undress himself, and he was asleep again the moment he lay down under the covers. As she lay in her bed, hearing below her the considerately low voices of the men in the parlor, their presence below her like depths to float upon, the sense of the loss of her son to the men seemed not so alarming, instead seemed desirable, for the presence of the men in the house, among them David, was to release her into a sleep that was like the expectation of a reward. The men came up quietly, their footsteps on the stairs a sound that in her half-sleep seemed to go on forever. She heard them in their rooms around her, the murmur of their voices, the scrape of a chair, and their number verified their strength. In each was the strength of all three and their strength was in David also, in his cot way up in the attic's vast reaches.

I I

Russell unlocked the door of the nightclub, fumbled on a light, and escorted her down red-carpeted stairs to a large, cold cellar where numerous little tables and chairs were scattered around a stage. The cellar ran under a restaurant and a bar, and the pipes along the ceiling were covered with a false sky—a black cloth painted with many gold moons, both crescent and round, and festooned with gilded gauze. The seepage and the dampness had been taken care of first, he told her; everything was as dry as a bone. The sign above the door—THE CARNIVAL—would be lit next Friday night, when the gossip columnists and some local big names would be wined and dined and entertained by a stripteaser and by a comedian and by a jazz trio who were to appear for the opening weeks. He himself, he said, and her father and the other owner had nothing to do with the details—everything from the plumbing to the entertainers was taken care of by the manager, but the whole works, he said, fascinated him. He did a jig step up on the stage, then stooped down to pick up a wire, and stood gazing upward to trace the origin of the trailing wire in his hand.

Later in the evening, in a quiet bar, he told her that he had been married twice, the first time when he was twenty. His second marriage had ended in the death of his wife, Anna. She had been a very unhappy person, weeping over slights that nobody else, he said, would even think to call slights, and, for days, brooding and miserable for reasons unknown to him. After a year she had decided to have a child because she might, she had said, feel necessary to somebody. But the child, a girl, had failed to bring that certainty to her and she had grown worse, calling herself foul names and wandering away, leaving the child alone in the house. She saw a psychiatrist almost every day, and every night took sedatives to sleep. She slept alone. The child slept in a bedroom of her own and he slept on the couch in the den. One night he was wakened by the smell of smoke and had time only to run into the child's room and rescue her. That part of the house where his wife slept was already in flames. Under the soft light of the bar lamps, he removed his coat, loosened a cuff link, and pushed up his shirtsleeve to show her the long, heavy scar down his arm.

The rest of the evening he brought up a hundred other topics, his way of apologizing for the story that had checked her vivacity. There was something unlikable about him after the story. She was afraid to be close with someone who had suffered the death of a wife under those circumstances. That he had been on the other side of the burning door, that he had been unable to break through, made it impossible for her to look into his eyes. She felt that he had been marked for that catastrophe and might be marked for others, and that there was nothing he could do to prevent them, even as he could not prevent his wife dying on the other side of the burning door. Yet, later in the night, lying with him in his apartment, she kissed the long scar on his arm, wondering if her dislike of him, earlier, had been fear of another dimension of reality. Waking in the middle of the night, she drank his brandy and laughed with him over a joke. When he sat up on the edge of the bed, she got up on her knees and kissed the back of his head and his shoulders, unwilling to let him go from her even for a moment, desiring to transform him, with her kissing, into a man who could avert any catastrophe.

The wedding, in the rectory of the church her mother attended, with only Russell's aunt and her parents and David present, seemed to her the wisest occasion of her life. Her parents liked him. He was a more responsive son, a more companionable son than their own; in addition, he was, at last, a son-in-law as affluent as they were, and perhaps more so.

They moved into a home he owned near Twin Peaks, on a wide avenue of white stucco homes of early California architecture. The lawn was perfect and so was the patio with its pink hydrangea bushes and granite birdbaths. The three of them, Russell and herself and David, each contributed, she felt, an admirable self to the pleasure of the marriage. At the beginning there appeared to be an easy compatibility between David and his stepfather, and their evenings together were always pleasant, with cocktails before supper and a special grenadine cocktail for David, and the gourmet suppers she cooked for them and for their frequent guests, Russell's friends, who were loan-company executives and bank officials, and their wives. They went on trips together in their red convertible to Lake Tahoe and to the mountains to fish and up into Sun Valley to ski, and always she was aware of the picture they made of the elegant family, climbing into or springing from their car and entering the lobby of the hotel, the father or the mother resting an arm on the boy's shoulder.

Neither she nor Russell had any desire to bring his daughter, Maria, to live with them, and, even had they wanted to, the girl would have chosen to remain with her maternal grandmother, a vigorous women with a daughter of seventeen, whom Maria idolized. They sometimes, however, took her along on their trips, and they sometimes had her over for a weekend, but her presence among them was, to Vivian, like a flaw in the picture. She was a year younger than David, a slight, colorless girl with enormous smoky blue eyes that seldom lifted. She was a reminder of the tragedy because it seemed to have shocked her from her normal pace of growth. When Russell brought the girl from her grandmother's, he hustled and bustled around to entertain her, to entertain them all. His eyes were tired when he came in the door with her, tired of the visit before it began, and afraid of the child he performed for. Around the girl he was a man making extravagant amends, a weary buffoon. In the last minutes of the girl's visits, with everybody collecting her possessions, gifts and hats and gloves and candy, Maria joined in with them, gave up sitting and being done unto, and, with her participation in the search, implied that she was both gratified and sorry her visit had roused them all to such a pitch of expiation.

After the girl's visits, when Vivian was left alone in the house with her son, there was always a time of relief, in which she felt the bond between herself and David, the bond of mother and son, to be stronger than that between herself and Russell. If Russell remained away, visiting with Maria's grandmother and, afterward, drinking at the nightclub, and David was asleep, she would go in and watch the boy while he slept.

In the light of lamp he lay on his back as if flung there, sometimes clear of the blankets from the waist up, his pajama top twisted upward, exposing his pale, tender stomach. He was, at these times, like an old friend. If her husband was not that, then her son was that. If marriage was not a resolving, then some compensation, or more than that, some answer, was to be found in the existence of her son. One night she bent and kissed him above the navel, pleased by the warm, resilient flesh, knowing that he would not wake up from the kiss because he slept so soundly and in the morning always came up fathoms out of sleep.

12

Some land that Russell had inherited south of the city, near the ocean, sold to a tract developer, and almost every week, or so it seemed to her, he sold at a great profit an old apartment building or a small hotel that he had bought only a few months before with a loan and had remodeled with another loan. And everything that she did with this prosperity brought words of praise, whether it was the accumulation of exquisite clothes or of oil paintings from the Museum of Art exhibits, the selection of silver and crystal and antiques, or the artistry of her suppers for a few guests. After two years in the house near Twin Peaks, they moved to a modern house surrounded by a Japanese garden, and the combining of her antiques with the modern architecture, all the harmonious combining was like a confirmation of the happiness of the family. It was further confirmed by color photographs in a magazine of interior decoration and by the article written by one of the editors who stressed the wonderful compatibility of antique and modern that had, as its source, the compatibility of the family with everything beautiful. No member of the family, however, appeared in the pictures—only Vivian at a far distance, her back turned, a very small figure in lemon-yellow slacks way out among the etching-like trees of the garden, glimpsed through the open glass doors of the living room. It was in bad taste to show the family, she understood; they would appear to be like the nouveaux riches, wanting to be seen among their possessions. Not to show the family gave more seclusion to the home and a touch of the sacred to the family.

In the second spring after their move to the new house, it was included in a tour of several beautiful homes in the city, the tour a charitable endeavor by the young matrons' league to which she belonged. While the woman who came once a week to the house was cleaning it the day before the tour, Vivian locked up in cabinets and closets small valuables that could be pocketed, although there was to be a leaguer in almost every room to act as hostess. It was customary for the owners of the houses in the tour to be away all day, and she had planned to spend the day with her mother, shopping for summer clothes. But the night before, carefully wiping out with a tissue the ashtrays she and Russell had been using and rinsing their liquor glasses, she knew she would remain in the house—not to hear words of praise and not to prevent any thefts, but to stand anonymously by and watch the flow of strangers who had paid their tour-ticket price in order to enter into the privacy of her home.

With the other women who were acting as hostesses, she awaited the invasion. Wearing a pink spring suit and white gloves, a white purse under her arm, she was, she felt, sure to be mistaken by the crowd for one of them. The early ones, at ten o'clock, entered with a reverent step because it was their first house of the day; but the later ones entered with less reverence, commenting loudly on plants and garden lamps as they came up the front path, taking in the living room with gazes already somewhat jaded by their acquaintance with other homes of secluded beauty. She watched them as she sat on the arm of a chair, chatting with a hostess, or wandered with them through the house. They were chic women, young and old, and they were impeccably dressed men with oblique faces as if seen in attendance upon her in a mirror of a beauty salon and never in direct confrontation; they were eccentrics, one a young woman in a garishly green outfit, with a pheasant feather a foot long attached to her beret and switching the space behind her as she stopped frequently, her feet in a dancer's pose, to glance around with large, transfixed eyes and a saintly smile; and there were two seedy brothers, shuffling and gray, who had the look of small-time realtors from the Mission district. For brief moments Vivian met eyes with the invaders, their roundly open eyes, their shifting eyes, their eyes ashamed of their curiosity, their envious eyes, and their eyes desiring ruin. She caught sight of a hole in the sock of one of the seedy brothers and of their run-down, polished shoes. She mingled with them up and down the hallways, on the flight of stairs between the two floors, and in and out of rooms, following a group into the serenity of the bedroom of herself and her husband and observing with them the wide, high-swelling bed, the ornately carved bedstead and the plum silk spread, the highboy with its shining brass hardware; the lamps, one on each side of the bed, a yard high with cylindrical shades of white silk; the black marble ashtrays; and the sand-color, thick carpeting that hushed everyone's step. They were fascinated by the small photos of Russell and David in pewter frames on her dressing table, and by a snapshot of the three of them in ski clothes. They bent to see the three faces closer, and after the others had done this, she, too, leaned closer to see for herself.

13

In the summer of the third year of their marriage they bought an old, large house near Clearlake on four acres planted with fruit trees. They invited two and three couples for weekends and spent the time in boats on the lake, over elaborate breakfasts and buffet suppers, drinking at the bars to survey the patrons and reclining at home in the sun or under the trees if the sun was too hot.

David was off on his own all day. He was twelve, that year, and although she knew that his distance from them all was due, in part, to a dislike of their friends, it was also, she felt, a sullen and almost violent resistance to any tracing of him, either the tracing of him in his roaming during the day or of his present self into the past, as the eyes of their friends traced him into childhood, and as hers did, and Russell's. They saw him cruising around on the lake with another boy in somebody else's motorboat, or laughing with another boy as the two bailed out a dinghy, or they did not see him for an entire day. Sometimes he did not come in for meals and ate leftovers up in his room, wanting more privacy than was given him in the kitchen where the guests went in and out and tried to talk with him.

One night, however, he came to watch them dance in their bare feet in the parlor. He sat on a kitchen chair near the door, his arms crossed over his chest and his legs stretched out toward the dancers. The women tugged at his shirt to persuade him to dance with them, and one drew up another chair by his and stroked his hair and called him shy. When at last he danced with the woman, he danced without the hesitation and clumsiness and deafness to the beat of the music that were signs of shyness. He danced with the woman almost instructively, a glide of insinuation in his hips and a contempt and an urging of her in his gaze that he kept on her belly and legs.

The night was warm, the house warmer than the night, containing in all its rooms the heat from the day. The women wore no more than they had worn during the day, cotton shorts and halters. The woman he was dancing with, the wife of the bank manager, had loosened her high pile of red hair so that it fell in strands along each side of her face. That she was short and stocky, that her long hair and bare feet made her almost comically squat, she was apparently not aware. They danced a foot apart, each flattering the other, seductively, with every move. The days of his avoiding them, of crossing to the other side of the road, of eating alone in his room at night—all were cast off in an eruption of melancholy desire. His eyes appeared almost black, they were open wider, and there was a firmness in his hands on the woman like that of a man experienced in arousing, and the vigor in his slender body ridiculed the men in the room who were slumped earthward, who were debilitated by the sun of the day rather than enlivened by it, as he appeared to be. Vivian recalled the comic dance he had performed as a child, the uncontrolled dancing, the stomping with no grace or rhythm, the prancing that was nothing more than self-tripping. The woman cupped her breast with one hand, a gesture that she did not appear conscious of. It must be, Vivian thought, a habitual caress, probably one that she gave herself when alone. The woman was smiling at David, and since he was watching her belly and legs, it appeared that she was watching herself with his eyes. When the music was over, she collapsed onto the couch, falling into her husband's lap.

"You ought to get him in the movies," said the bank manager. His hands had gone up to protect himself from his wife's falling body; in the next moment he had removed his hands from her, jerking his leg away also. He was a tall thin man whose high, complaining voice Vivian would often hear when she stood in the marble rotunda of the bank, and once she had watched him stride from his carpeted enclosure, slam the gate that only swung noiselessly, and run up the stairs, too impatient and full too of complaints to wait for the slow elevator.

"You remember that kid? You remember that thirteen-year-old kid?" Duggan, an attorney, a small, blond man who wore sports clothes that seemed with their expensiveness to dwarf him. Even when his lips were not moving in speech, they moved with anticipation of speech. "You remember he ran away with that woman? I attended the hearing. She had six kids and was thirty-eight and I forgot to mention she had a husband too. They took her 1941 Plymouth to Tucson and shacked up there in a motel—Big Indian or Little Indian Motel—stayed for four days, I think it was, before they were apprehended. She said she loved him, she said she loved him more than her husband, she said he was the greatest lover of the century. One of her boys was two and a half years older than her lover. She was stacked, that woman, almost six feet tall. You can imagine." He was talking rapidly and loudly over the music of the record that had dropped into place.

Vivian turned the volume knob to obliterate his moist voice and, dancing, approached her son. She danced with him in a spontaneous attempt to prove to all of them that his dancing was a boy's imitation of dancing he had seen in the movies and that he was ignorant of its implications. She was a shield between him and the lascivious attorney's story. But he lost his competence dancing with her; his legs bungled the rhythm, he looked down at his feet, and when the music was over he sat apart again.

When David danced with Duggan's wife, who came up to him, he made up with wildness for his clumsiness dancing with his mother. The woman was a tall blonde, with utter vanity in the poking forward of her gaunt hips and long, bare thighs; an assumption, in her dancing postures, of a lunacy that matched her partner's. These women had no lunacy, Vivian thought. They had no wantonness, no risk, and he was wasting on them his abandonment of himself to his sensuality, the first public display of the sensuality that would be his in years to come. With her back to the dancing couple, with her drink held up high in her right hand while with her left she riffled through the record albums on the table, she lifted her eyes to see their reflection in the French doors: the woman's turquoise shorts and white blouse with its one diagonal stripe of red, her long bare arms and legs in angular seduction, and David's small figure in tan pants and soiled white shirt, his dark hair, and his face that was pale in the reflection against the night and yet was brown from the summer sun—both figures moving across the panes to the blaring jangle of the music.

At the moment she turned to watch them, Russell slipped himself between David and the woman, holding his arms up high in exaggerated homage to her and dancing away with her in his small-footed way that was always just a beat off. David sat for a while watching them, then went upstairs while everyone was dancing. After he left, although the records continued to fall into place and the music blared on and the vocalists sang on or whispered on, there was no more dancing.

Russell mixed a drink for them all that he called a golden viper. "This'll stone you on the first swallow," he warned them. The bank manager's wife sipped with a little girl's curiosity, her eyes big over the rim of her glass. Russell, Vivian saw, made the most of this small sway over them; from the secret of the viper he went on to reveal another secret—where and for what a low price he had purchased the cut glass from which they drank, holding up his glass to the light and turning it in his fingers, conscious, she knew, that she was watching him critically. While he sat on the edge of the table, the center of the group, host and entertainer, she remembered the times she had driven him home after parties, listening while he incoherently probed his depths and deplored his friends' shallowness. The loan officials who peopled his days, he condemned when alone with her. They respected him for what they called his genius, and their appraisers overvalued the hotels and apartment houses so that the loans they made to him were larger than warranted; he ate lunch with them in the best restaurants and drank with them in the best bars, and was, she knew, always his charming, boyish, shrewd, and witty self; and at night he ridiculed them for a tie, for suede shoes, and for their very shrewdness that saw him as the one to put their money on.

While they were talking about the war in Korea, with the bank manager predicting that the Chinese were going to overrun the world, Vivian left them and went up the stairs. The heat of the day was pocketed in the upstairs hallway; all the bedroom doors, and David's door at the end of the hallway, were closed. He was lying under the sheet, the blankets thrown off onto the floor, reading under the metal lamp fixed to the bed. His head was tilted against the headboard, the pillow stuffed under his neck.

"You were the life of the party and now they're just talking," she told him, collapsing into the canvas chair and resting her feet on the bed. The room had a meager look; it was more a sanctum than his room at home. "Silly rug looks like it's eaten all around the edge by mouse teeth," she said, lowering one leg to kick up the edge of the rug. "Read a little to me," she said, closing her eyes.

"It's just about birds," he said.

"Go on, read to me if it's about birds," she urged. "I'm interested in birds."

"What part?" he asked, embarrassed, she saw, about reading aloud, knowing that her interest was feigned. He flipped through the pages to lose deliberately the page that he had been reading, leading her away from himself by leading her away from the part that had absorbed him. "The hummingbird can't glide," he said. "You want that important bit of information?"

"Ah, poor things, can't glide," she said. "Go on. But what do they need to glide for?"

"You act like a teacher," he said. "They ask you questions and spoil everything."

"Me a teacher?" she cried in mock distress. "I came

in here to learn a few things and you accuse me of acting like a teacher. Baby, I'm ignorant," she pleaded. "I don't know anything about birds except they've all got feathers and go peep-peep. Go on and tell me about them. Because birds are the greatest miracle. God really outdid Himself when He made a bird. Say you and I were God, could we think up something like a bird? Never in a million years. It took God to think them up, and even for Him it was something. You go on, tell me more about birds."

"It says about migration," he began again, "that millions of them never get there, where they're going. It says it's really a big risk to a bird, the biggest risk in his life. It says that hundreds of millions of them never get there."

"Isn't that funny? I thought they all made it," she said.

For a time he read to her about the perils of migration. She recrossed her ankles, while she listened, observing the arches of her bare feet. Then, because she heard a murmur of voices in the glassed-in porch below, where the bank manager and his wife slept, and knew that the rest would be coming up the stairs and that only a short time was left her in her son's room, she lost her feigned reverence for birds. "Listen, Davy baby," she began. "I don't want you to get vain about being a good dancer or looking like the great lover Gable just because you stirred up those women down there. You're neither. You want to know what it is?" She tilted her head back, lifting her gaze to the ceiling. "It's your youth. It's because you're so young, baby." She laughed. "You look at them as if you're seeing women for the first time, and what it does to them is make them feel they're being seen for the first time by any man. You make them feel fabulous—oh, as if they've got a thousand secrets they could tell you." She laughed again, still toward the ceiling. "You know what Russell is going to say? When everybody is asleep, he'll say in a whisper, he'll say, 'Davy got out of hand tonight, didn't he? Those women will be creeping around the house all night long.'" She brought her gaze down, a humorously warning gaze. "You want to put a chair against your door?"

She saw in his expressionless face that he did not want to understand her joke. He did not want to suspect that she had come up the stairs and away from the others not to tell him about the other women but to tell him, by her presence, that nobody else could claim his enticing youth except herself, if it were to be claimed at all. He was her son; she had given him his life and his youth, his present and his future, his elusiveness, and, by telling him she knew his effect upon the other women, she was reminding him of her claim to him, if she had a claim. "Go on," she said, settling farther into her chair. "Read to me, read to me."

She heard Duggan and his wife come up the stairs and enter their bedroom quietly, while the murmuring below was borne out on the still air into the dark yard. After a time she heard Russell come up. Then the murmuring ceased and the house was silent. David read to her for a while longer and when he was tired of reading she told him to turn off the light, and she sat in darkness, reluctant to go to her husband, to lie down beside him. She was struck by the years of her accumulated contempt for her husband as by an unexpected blow to her body. Their voices muted by the darkness, she and her son talked together, finding inconsequential things to talk about. He told her about a boy he had made friends with a few days before and how far around the lake they went with the boy's uncle in his motorboat, and as he talked she listened more to the sound of his voice than to the words, feeling the sound of his young voice, his faltering, low, slightly hoarse voice reverberate in her body.

Her husband was sitting on the bed in the darkness. The light from the hallway, as she opened the door, revealed him half undressed, smoking a cigarette. Though he was not yet in bed, he had already turned off the lamp, or not turned it on, apparently wanting to reject her with darkness, and she felt that she had come from the presence of a man who was more than he. It seemed to her that Russell and the others in the house and herself were all to be left behind by her son, their lives nothing compared to what his life was to be, that this man, castigating her with darkness, sat in a cul-de-sac of a life. She felt that all of them except her son were trapped in the summer night in that house with the unwashed glasses and ashtrays on floors and couches and windowsills, with intimate, used garments on floors and chairs—everything testifying to wasted lives.

"Golden vipers," she said, low, pacing the floor in her bare feet, making no noise on the floorboards, as if she were weightless. "Always some little surprise or other, always some concoction nobody ever heard of before and that's deadly familiar. How do you manage to accomplish both at the same time?"

"Enough, enough. Every little thing. Enough . . . ," he said, breathing out the words as if someone were testing him physically to see how much pain he was able to bear.

"They all add up to the big thing."

"What's the big thing?" he asked, challengingly, unafraid.

"You. They all add up to you." She was unable to move, struck by her own cruelty.

"You don't see me right, Vivian," he said. "You've got a crazy way of looking at me. You put together things nobody notices because they're nothing to notice. You watch for everything and call it a fault."

She pressed her temples to destroy the cruelty in her head, but it was not cornered by a posture or a wish. "It's you I see," she insisted.

"Me? Me?" He kept his voice low. "You act like I misrepresented myself. I never misrepresented myself, Vivian. Besides, you're smart, Vivian. You're smart enough to know if a man's lying to you. That's not saying I'm satisfied with myself. You don't know what's plaguing me. You think I think everything's great.

You think I think my life's just great. What I gripe about—this guy and that guy, some deals—you think there's nothing else that gripes me. I see the way you see me and I don't look so good, sometimes, but you can't see what I *feel*. I'd like to tell you what I feel. Or maybe I wouldn't like to. If I could tell you, you still wouldn't know." He paused. "I'll tell you," and paused again. He was rubbing his knees, trying to rub away his confusion over himself, straining to engage his being in whatever was the aspiration he could not find words for.

It was so amorphous a thing for him to tell—the thing which he hoped would make him more in her eyes—that the attempt to reveal it was almost like an attempt to confess a crime instead of to reveal a virtue.

She went over to him. There was no one else to lie down beside if she wanted an embrace against her own cruelty. He leaned forward to clasp her around her legs, drawing her down with him.

"Vivian, listen. When I first saw you, the way you ran down that hill like a kid, I said there's a woman with a heart as big as the world. So if I blow up, you're supposed to know I don't mean it. Lie still, lie still," he urged.

14

Maria came to visit more frequently at Vivian's invitation until she was with them almost ritually every weekend. Along with the diffidence, there was now in her manner almost the slyness of a spy in the enemy camp. At twelve she was ineffectually pretty in Vivian's eyes; there was no quickness, no grace, no wiles, no artifice to make persuasive the large, smoky blue eyes and fair skin; and this lack of conscious femininity, which was, to Vivian, the very soul of a woman, was not, she thought, the girl's fault, not the dead mother's fault, not the fault of the grandmother with whom she lived, but Russell's fault. The girl was evidence to her always that he had not been the man he ought to have been in that other marriage. The girl was like the dead wife's past consciousness of him as he was; she was like the wife's dismayed, sorrowing consciousness of him.

With the girl, they drove up to the mountains to ski, and Maria, who could not ski and could not learn, spent the time walking in snowshoes, and Vivian sometimes accompanied her, affected by the sight of the girl alone, her sad face surrounded by a knit cap of exultant red. In the summer, they drove to Monterey, or up into the gold-mining country and gambled on the machines in desolate saloons, or they went to Clearlake or to Tahoe to swim.

Constantly urged by Russell to intrude upon David, to swim as far, to climb as far, Maria, one day at Lake Tahoe, in the midst of Russell's badgering, stood up from the shallow water where she had been paddling around and struck out after David, who was climbing onto a raft several yards offshore. She was an awkward swimmer, fearful and rigid. Even so, while they watched apprehensively and with shame, the girl, apparently propelled by sheer anger against the man who had taunted her, got as far as midway, and then could neither turn back nor continue on to the raft. Russell ran into the water and swam after her, and, with one arm around her, helped her back to shore. Once on her feet and out of the water, Maria refused to go as far as the blanket where they had congregated before. She sat down on wet sand, facing the water, clasping her knees, not acknowledging her father's presence or Vivian's. Vivian laid a sweater over the girl's back and sat down beside her. Russell lay on his back, several yards away.

"I think he wanted me to drown," Maria said.

"That's not true." Vivian put her arm around the girl.

"It's true," the girl said.

"But he rescued you."

"I wasn't drowning."

"Then you see, it's not true," Vivian said, hugging the girl to impress upon her their humorous reasoning.

Maria sat alone, after Vivian had left her, until it was time for them to leave the lake, and on the long drive back to the city that evening she did not speak, not even to answer.

Russell returned at two in the morning, after taking Maria home, and, as was his habit, stopping by at the nightclub. He stumbled down onto the bench of Vivian's dressing table, facing her where she lay in bed. "You terribly awfully fond of her, Vivian?" he asked. "Why?"

"Why?" she repeated, half asleep.

"Why?"

"Why? Because I guess I feel sorry for her."

"You're not fond of her and you're not sorry for her and you're not fond of me and you're not sorry for me. You just don't like me. It's that simple. That's the crux of it. You don't like me and because you don't like me you fix it up so we see her every week. You use her to remind me of something you think ought to be plaguing me. What do you want to plague me with, Vivian?" He began to weep without covering his face, and his pale eyes, paler because of the deeply flushed face, seemed to have wept out their color before he returned home to weep.

She slept in the guest room after that night, and

heard him come home, stumbling, slamming doors, an hour after the nightclub closed. One night he did not come home, and in the morning her father telephoned to tell her that the manager had ordered Russell from the club because he had made a nuisance of himself, complaining to the patrons that his wife refused to sleep with him. He did not come home that day and, at two in the morning, her father telephoned again: Russell had spent the evening in the restaurant next door to the club, buying drinks for a couple, buying supper for them, telling of his ostracism, that his wife forbade him to come home and his partners forbade him to enter the nightclub.

An hour after her father had called, Russell returned. "It's me, don't shoot!" he shouted, unlocking the front door. "Vivian, you hear me up there? I'm turning on all the lights so you can see it's me. You saw that thing in the papers? She shot her husband dead because she thought he was a prowler?" He came up the stairs, stamping, and into their bedroom, shaking his keys above his head with both hands.

As if he felt he required some excuse for being there, for returning, he began to undress, pulling at his tie, unbuttoning his shirt before he had removed his coat. He took off his coat and seemed surprised to find his tie gone and his shirt already unbuttoned. Then, as if he were afraid that somebody else had unbuttoned him because he was incapable of it, because he was drunk, his face flushed up in humiliation. "What's this guilt every woman puts on me? What's this bloody guilt?" he shouted. "What're you retaliating for, Viv? What're you retaliating for? You're always retaliating for something I never know I do to you."

"I said nothing," she said.

"You say nothing. What makes you think you need to say something? I get the point. And Maria says nothing, but I get the point. She's like a creditor—I didn't pay my bill, I didn't meet my obligations, or the check bounces. What's this guilt every woman puts on me? What's this bloody guilt? I been walking around with it all my life. I was sitting next to this guy and I was telling him what a wonderful woman you are and goddamn how I didn't deserve you, how I wasn't good enough for you, when he says to me, 'You got guilt on you, man. What you don't deserve is your guilt.' That man, a stranger, knows more about me than any man I call a friend. 'You got guilt on you,' he says. 'That's the only thing you don't deserve.' You hear that? Seems to be a goddamn disease that women got. They give you a dose of guilt like a whore gives you a dose of clap." He sat down on the bench, bent over to untie his shoe, his face lifted to her at the same moment that his bare back was reflected in the large, round mirror of the dressing table, and it seemed to her that his undressing was an act assuring him his words would not, after all, bring about the end. "If there were trials, if there were trials, if they could accuse you of leading your wife to her end just by being yourself, they'd do it and hang you for it. Isn't that the truth, over there? That you got me for life and what kind of life is it? You got everything invested in me and who am I? What I'd like to know is why the hell did you get into the bind? And why the hell did Anna? Why did *she?* What do you want? What do you expect? You think you're embracing the whole goddamn universe and you wake up the next morning and it's me there? It's me there? And what do you do, then? You give me this guilt. You give me this guilt when I'm spitting up my heart to do the job right."

She threw off the covers and sat on the edge of the bed, trembling. Alerted by her movement, apparently suspecting that she was about to flee across the hall to her son, he lifted his head as if he could, if he tried, hear David listening. The boy could not hear the words, she knew, but the angry pitch could reach him. "You get 'em young enough, you got 'em on your side. You get 'em in the cradle. That's it. That's a goddamn political truth, every politician knows that. Give 'em the ideology with their mother's milk and you got 'em for life. Go on in and throw yourself on him and tell him what you're suffering, tell him how I make you suffer." He slammed his hand down hard and flat on the bench. "I never did anything to you!" he shouted. "I never did anything to any woman that I have to feel guilty about. Why do you want to make me guilty?"

"I'm not Anna," she said. "Don't talk to me that way," as if he had shouted that other wife into her grave.

"You're all Anna," he cried. "You're all alike. Sometimes I start to call you Anna." He stood up to unbuckle his belt but the rage against her forced him to put on his shirt again. His hands shook as they went down the buttons.

She began to walk around the room, frightened by his accusation that she was as his wife Anna had been. She had not thought that the desperation in herself was as much as in that other woman, but this comparing them roused in her the fear that it was as much. "If I'm Anna," she cried, "then I can tell you how she felt. You want to know how she felt? Everything she said against herself was against you, because she was afraid to say it against you."

"She wasn't afraid to say it!" he shouted. "What makes you think she was afraid?"

"Sometimes I say it, but I'm afraid when I say it," she told him. "Every time I say something against you to your face, it's like a terrible falling, like I've cut the ground out from under my feet."

"That *is* the ground under your feet!" he shouted. "That *is* the ground."

"No, it's true," she said, twining her fingers. "It's true what I say. That's the way she felt, I *know*. She couldn't bear you anymore, but she couldn't cut the ground away. That's a terrible thing, not to be able to bear the ground under your feet. What do you do then but die?"

"You blame me for it?"

She gave him a look of scorn, and was appalled by the slipping away of the ground. He came toward her and she waited, unable to expect that he would strike her. He struck her and she fell to her knees, clinging to him. He grasped her arms and flung her off. When she got to her feet, he followed her. "Go on! Goddamn! Go on! Go on, faster!" he shouted. "You know the way, you know the way. Take off your goddamn nightgown. What's that on for when you run naked in the hall-way? He'll think you're dressed to go out, looks like a goddamn dress to go out in." He grasped the hem of it, but she swung around, striking at him, and, missing him, fell against her son's door.

Above her, she saw her son strike Russell in the chest. The boy flew at the man, all his taciturnity released into rage, into shouting and striking. Russell flung him away, and when the boy fell against the wall, struck him in the face with the back of his hand and left them. David helped her into his room and locked the door, and they sat together on his bed, trembling, listening to Russell's sobs and his screams at the sobs to stay down, and they heard the rush of water in the basin. Then he left the house, raced the engine of his car, and roared away.

She ran down the stairs and bolted the door, afraid that he would return, afraid that later in the night, wher-ever he was, in some hotel room, he would be forced to return. She lay down in her bed. She was not concerned with her son; he could take care of himself and his own wounds. If he was trembling, it was with fear of things beginning, of woundings and conflicts beginning; he was not trembling with the fear of endings.

15

In the morning they packed a few clothes and left the house, wanting to be away if Russell returned. On the drive down to Monterey, David drowsed in the sun beating into the open car, his head lolling back against the seat. She glanced at his face; as dearly familiar as it was, she always found more than a touch of the unfamiliar, and now the bruise increased the strangeness. As she drove with the drowsing boy, it seemed to her that his elusiveness was an accusation that she had always, since his birth, held other persons to be more valuable than he, that all her time was spent in the company of other persons for whom she must make herself valuable, when who were the others, after all? He was to repay her in kind, she knew. It was inevitable. He was to spend his life in the company of persons whose value for him she would never be able to comprehend, and she felt a deep stirring of curiosity about that life of his beyond his fourteen years and about those persons, some not yet born, who were to rake his mind and his heart with their being.

On either side of the highway stretched rows of low, tangled vines, their green muted by the fine dust concocted of hot sun and vast open fields. For miles she drove through sun-bleached hills, ranging in color from almost white to a dark gold, and early in the afternoon she turned along by the sea. Her body felt fragile, but the sun on her bare arms and legs and on the crown of her head was a healing warmth. They found a pink stucco motel, primly neat, fronted by geometrical patches of grass and gravel, and ringed by cypress. The walls of the room were coral pink and the spreads on the twin beds were also coral, scrawled with white nautical designs. They left their cases on the beds and walked to the restaurant close by, whose enormous sign was like a lighted tower signaling ships at sea.

She walked in, aware of their complementary beauty, the young mother and her young son, both pretending an easy familiarity with the place, although his pretense, she knew, was the result of shyness. He walked behind her, yet she knew, from having turned other times in other restaurants to ask him something, just how he looked, how one thumb was hooked in his back pocket and how he glanced neither to the right nor to the left but kept his gaze down to the level of her ankles.

She was glad to see that there were waiters here and no waitresses, and to their young waiter she made evident her consciousness of him as a man in the way she rested her elbow on the table and set her profile on view, and in the way she took a cigarette from her purse and smiled at him to light it for her. She shared her graces between the waiter and her son who, because of his attack on Russell, had made the unspoken demand of him to treat him as the man he was to become; and, afraid of that demand, she required an obvious flirtation with the waiter, almost an infatuation. The waiter's eyes wobbled away when their glances met. He told them, as he picked up soup bowls and laid down salad bowls, keeping his elbows close to his sides, that the weather yesterday had been very nice, the sun up hot and early. It was time, he said, for the fog to roll in. "Is there any fog on the horizon?" he asked, like one denied the sight of the day, although the restaurant's front windows looked out to sea. She reported that they had seen no fog, nothing, and laughed with the waiter over his moody refusal to glance out the window at the clear day that others were free to roam around in.

The tide was out when they strolled down to the water, so far out it left exposed a wide stretch of wet sand reflecting the sandpipers running over it. With his trouser legs rolled up, gesturing widely, David told her that the water was drawn far out like that before a tidal wave. He seemed elated by the prospect. She walked in step with him over the firm wet sand and through cool gusts of wind raised by the breakers. The flock of sandpipers rose up incredibly swift, skimming over the waves, turning so fast in one instant, flashing white, then dark. Far up the beach, the flock curved in again and landed. On the horizon lay a slate-blue bank of fog.

"You want to bet tomorrow is foggy?" she said, hugging herself against the thought of it. "There's nothing more dreary than fog by the ocean. Let's go to the mountains somewhere. Let's do that."

Once they had canceled their room, however, and carried their bags to the car, her desire to leave the town grew less and they spent several hours wandering the streets where the smart shops were, and they stayed on to eat a late supper out on the wharf. On the drive to the Santa Cruz mountains, he talked awhile about the day's trivia, uneasy, she knew, over his changing voice; then he was silent. She asked him if he were awake and heard no reply, but she suspected that the night and their aloneness for miles forced him to dissemble sleep.

It was past midnight when she drove into the parking area of a cabin motel, and whether he had slept for hours or had fallen asleep a moment before they arrived, he woke up only long enough to carry in his overnight bag and to undress and climb into bed. She switched off the paper-shaded lamp that stood on the small table between the beds and undressed by the yard light. She lay with her back to him and the room, her gaze on the vine that webbed the screen high in the wall, afraid to move, afraid that the small sound of the turning of her body would be enough to wake him.

16

The morning was hot and filled with the chitter of birds. David was already gone from the room when she awoke; she heard him talking in the yard with a woman. She peered out through the screen. The yard was struck with sun, a shock of white space in which she could not locate him.

They ate their breakfast at a cafe near the motel and took the trail suggested to them by the proprietor, climbing up through the silence of the day that seemed to resound off the mountains in waves. Small lizards ran off the narrow trail into the dry grass, stopping to lift their heads and look back. David kept his eyes on a large bird circling so that he could name it for her; but it soared away as if it were swept off to the side by some wide current of heat. When she climbed ahead of him, he darted side to side so that his voice could reach around her, and when she came along behind him, he paused on the trail to turn and tell her something to her face, and sometimes he walked backwards. A dog was barking down below, and the sound was isolated by the silence, and magnified and like another sound, a sound she had never heard before, the barking of a beast that went by the name of dog. This discovery of the unfamiliar in the dog's barking set off an elation in her breast. A delight in the preposterous. And she was delighted with herself for running away from her husband, for running away from her marriage, for running away from everything that bound her.

She stepped off the trail into a clearing and sat down on a rock in the scanty shade of a tree, counting on the prosaic act of resting and smoking a cigarette to bring her down to the prohibitive world again. A long time ago someone had begun to erect a cabin in the clearing and had given up. Around them lay rusty chains and saw blades, a mound of yellow newspapers, pulpy and mixed with the gray stuffing of a moldy mattress; and the giving up, after hauling up the trail the materials of the future, was further cause for the ridiculous elation that the barking of the dog had set off. The sun was directly overhead, the shade was not enough, and the sweat ran down from under her breasts to where her shorts were belted in. David had taken off his shirt and was wiping his chest and face with it. Up in the tallest tree an insect was making a ringing noise, a high-pitched humming like a sound of torment, as though the sun was slowly burning its edges away.

David spoke to her, but all she heard was the waiting silence after his voice. She wanted him to know her body again as he had known it as an infant or to know her body as he had not known it, like a lover who had been unconscious of who it was he had loved, who had loved a woman for a time and yet not known the person she was; and she wanted to know his body as she had known it and claimed it when he was an infant and as it would be in the years to come when he was apart from her, and she wanted this knowledge of each other to put them forever apart from everyone else, as covertly wise persons were apart. She glanced over at him as he leaned against a tree two yards away from her. Gazing at her, he looked stricken and pale in the sun, like someone waiting to be sacrificed. She ground her cigarette into the dirt. There were dry pine needles and rust-colored leaves on the ground, and as though she were concerned about starting a blaze, she continued to grind the cigarette with the sole of her shoe, sending all the wanting down into the earth.

They went down the trail to the highway, he following her from afar. On the edge of the highway, as they walked together again, unspeaking, she placed her hand on his shoulder, needing to assure herself that she had meant him no harm.

In the motel swimming pool, in the midst of countless children, she was kicked by beating feet, water splashed in her eyes and shouts rang in her ears, and she dodged small, sharp elbows. She often lost sight of him; once saw him talking to a girl a year or two older than he, both of them holding to the edge of the pool and with only their heads above water. The girl's light brown hair in wet strands to the shoulders, the small, delicate profile, the unformed and forming spirit, brought her a moment's anguish. Surrounded by splashing young bodies, she suspected that if she were to drown she would not be missed, that she would lie at the bottom of the pool, and for hours, for the entire day under the sun, the young bodies would splash above her. Even when her body was discovered she would not be missed. So now, in the time before she was drowned, in the time before the water seeped under her cap and the chlorine turned her bleached hair green and she became a grotesque drowned woman, in the time before she was dead and revealed, she must experience a union with him that was more than with any other person on earth. It was not enough to have given him birth, it was not enough to be his mother, that union was not enough. Mothers were always of the past and never of the future. A boy rose straight up out of the water directly in front of her, bumping against her legs and breasts. For a second he looked at her with bright, unseeing eyes; then he struck away from her and was at once lost among the other shrill and splashing children. Frightened, she climbed from the pool, away from all the quick, contemptuous bodies in the water.

When she had dressed, she walked down the highway to the cafe. She slipped a morning paper from the rack and was opening it to read at the counter while she drank her coffee when David got onto the stool beside her, his body wet, his bare feet coated with the dust of the highway. Unspeaking, they ate side by side, he with his back humped and his head bent down, and shivering a little. Some water ran down his temple, some dripped from his trunks to the floor. She was pleased with his alarm—it was like an outburst, a confession—and at the same time she was afraid of it and of the pleasure that she took in it.

While he put on his clothes, she waited for him in the yard, and they walked for miles along the highway, past motels and cabins and streams. Not only the exercise but the immense, vertical, judicial monotony of the forest was tiring. She saw the forest as austere and disinterested, but she knew that, if they were to rest again among the trees, the judicial aspect would dissolve within the heat and the silence.

On the way back they ate supper at a small restaurant in another motel, sitting at a green Formica table; then they returned to their cabin and lay down on their beds, flat on their backs, with their dusty shoes still on. The air was cool with the onset of evening and the yard light in the trees began to filter into the room as the twilight deepened. He slipped off her sandals and tucked around her feet the Indian blanket that lay folded at the foot of the bed. After taking off his shoes he lay down again on his bed, watching her. In the yard a group of guests were talking together. She knew by their voices and laughter who they were— provincials, churchgoers, probably off a tour bus.

"Sounds like a bunch of fools," she said. She sat up, lit a cigarette, and, leaning back against the wall, with the red glass ashtray on her lifted knees, she comically mimicked the voices, the cackling laughter, attempting to destroy the importance of the ones who saw no reason within the unreasonable and who never forgave an aberration. But she knew that her ridicule would fail if only because she wanted it to fail. She wanted those densely stolid persons out in the yard to interfere. They were judges, a convocation of judges.

David lay gazing at her, absorbed by the suspect interplay of her low voice with their loud ones. When the group wandered away, she got up, covered him with a blanket, then lay down again under her own blanket. Later in the night she heard him undressing in the dark and lying down again. A wind was rising, rattling twigs against the roof, and she fell asleep within the mingling of darkness and wind and trees.

17

They returned to the city in the morning and found the house unlocked and all her husband's belongings gone. He had taken nothing more than his personal possessions—his clothes and his papers and his few books on real estate and his skis, but all that was left, everything that belonged to the house and to her, was less, as if most of the intrinsic value was gone. After a few days, this devaluation of the objects passed and she began to cherish each one as if each were proof of her attempt to build a sound and lasting marriage. She polished silver, fine wood, and brass, and when everything was polished and the settlement arrived at—after hours in her attorney's office haggling with Russell's attorney—and the house and its furnishings hers and the divorce filed, she was again alienated from the house. Each time a man was gone from her life she felt that the time with him had deprived her of all sorts of possibilities with another, with others.

She felt that she had forfeited another kind of life for herself.

In the fall David began his first year in high school. Often he did not return home until a few minutes before supper, and after supper he wandered out again. She began going out to parties, as much to be with her friends as to avoid her son's avoidance of her, and sometimes she was the last to leave a party, coming home in the early morning.

With her cousin Teresa she opened a shop where imported craft was sold—brassware from India, sweaters from Sweden, glass from Mexico, something from almost everywhere. The shop was located in a block of other small, high-class shops—a florist and an interior decorator and a designer of chic maternity clothes. Sitting in a crimson sling chair all day, reading paperbacks, she was more bored than she had ever been in her life. With a graceful gliding down of her hands to pick up an object for a customer, with a graceful cupping of the object, stroking it as if it were alive, she attempted to engross herself in the shop, in the objects tinkling and glittering, fragile, transparent, iridescent, gilded. But the attempt failed, and she sold her interest and looked for another occupation to keep her away from the house and to engage her.

She served as a volunteer saleswoman in a shop operated by the young matrons' league to which she belonged; clothes discarded by wealthy women were sold there at very low prices and the proceeds given over to charity. The hours dragged while she fended off, with her cigarettes and mint chocolates, the stale smell of the place, of the dry-cleaned clothes mixed with the smell of shop dust. One afternoon, alone, she found the staleness unbearable. The staleness had got into the nice, clean garments that hung in rows under discarded prints of van Gogh and Currier & Ives and Chagall, also for sale; the staleness was in the shoes, worn to the shape of the past owners' feet and whitened or blackened, and with new rubber heels; the staleness was in the thin carpet whose colors and pattern were worn down to a drab gray; it was in the table on which her elbows rested, the scars evident under the coat of chartreuse paint. It seemed to her that the staleness had been present in the garments even while they were being worn by whoever had bought them first, and that it was present in everything that covered the body or decorated the house because, soon enough, the dress and the vase and the rug and the necklace would all belong to the past. A light, cold rain was falling; the Chinese paper lantern with its silk tasseled cord, hanging from the ceiling, shook a little, and the wind suddenly banged against the door with the weight of a falling body. She put on her raincoat and locked the door.

By taxi she went up the hill to the Mark Hopkins hotel and, after ordering a drink in the bar off the lobby, she telephoned the man she had spent the night with two nights before, a married man who kept an apartment of his own as a condition for remaining with his wife and two children. She wanted desperately to lie with him in the afternoon while others were at work, while others engaged in their acts of charity, while everything went on that always went on. She required his need of her in an hour when he ought to be engaged in something else, in whatever was the protocol, the ritual, the complexity of his occupation; she required the certainty that she had persuaded him to come to her for that hour and to postpone all else.

"So I ran out," she said, leaning back against the wall of the booth, her voice down low in her throat, her mouth close against the phone. "Let me tell you I couldn't get out of that smelly place fast enough. I felt like I was smothered."

"Listen, Viv," he interrupted. "I'm snowed under here."

"Me too, me too. Nicky, love, I know just how you feel." She was unable to let him go, unable to get set for the plunge down into panic. "Listen, can you drop everything for a minute and come up here? I mean we can go and sit at the top, if you want, and watch the rain come down on the roofs way down beneath us. Don't you think that'd be exciting?"

"I can't," he said, his voice impersonal suddenly. "I'd love to, but I can't."

"Well, if you'd *love* to, you've got to do it," she said. "Think of all the opportunities you've had in your life to do the things you'd love to do and didn't do. I met a man the other night whose brother just threw everything over and went to Tahiti. Thriving, really, a canning executive, just like you, only in St. Louis, can't remember, or Iowa, and never came back. Got six mistresses over there, no seven, and all that beautiful scenery. If you'd try and make a list of all the things you let yourself miss, you couldn't, you'd break right down and cry. Go on, start making your list. You don't have to write it down, just make it in your head. Go on." She gave him a few seconds and felt the loss of the hour, of the man, of whatever value she wanted him to impart to her with his acquiescent desire. "Listen, if you don't want a drink, you might want to do something else," she said, afraid that he had not understood the reason for her call. "You might want a different kind of break in the middle of the day. You want to go up to your place? You want to meet me there?"—trying with her husky voice, with the murmurous volition of her voice, to convince him of his need of her at that hour.

"There's nothing I'd like better," he said. "But there's nothing I can do about it."

"Nicky, baby. Baby, you there?" she pleaded, her voice like her voice in his ear or over his body.

"Viv," he begged.

"Listen, baby, I'll die if you don't," she said. "I'll pass out in the lobby here. That's what they pass out from, those women you see passing out in lobbies. They tell you—I mean when they're carried off and revived—they tell you they just had a tooth extracted or they ate something, but they're lying. They die of what you're doing to me."

"Viv, where are you?" he asked, when she was silent.

"You haven't been listening. The first thing I said to you," she reminded him, "was, 'Nicky, baby, I'm at the Mark.'"

"You want a taxi home?" he asked. "I'll call you a taxi to take you home."

"Nobody was ever so good to me!" she cried. "Like sit way over in his office and call me a taxi way over here. God, you have no idea what that means to me. Nobody ever."

"Viv, come off it," he begged.

"You know what I think of a man who puts a woman in a taxi? I don't care whether he's right there on the curb or a mile away. The man who puts a woman in a taxi and turns around and walks the other way has got no intimation of what's going to become of her. He doesn't know and he doesn't care. That's what I think of a man who calls you a taxi."

"Vivian, for the love of God, hang up," he pleaded. "So I don't have to hang up on you."

"Say uncle," she said.

"Oh God—uncle."

She went back to her table in the bar and sat very erect on the banquette, flushed with shame. She lived, as she had learned a long time ago, by delusion and desperation, but there was nobody worth the agony, no man, not even God, nobody worth the desperation to entice and to impress, nobody worth the delusion that she was invaluable to him and he invaluable to her. She ordered another drink, caressing the back of the waiter's hand when he set it down before her. They were friends, she knew him by name, and she knew he was prepared, if she glanced up, to wink at her consolingly. When the glass was empty, she put on her raincoat with the waiter's help and went out through the lobby to where the taxis came in under the canopy.

She called to her son from the doorstep, her harsh voice grating her throat. She had no idea of what she would do with her anger if he were home; perhaps strike him across the back as she had done that once when he was a small child, strike him with her fists while he hung his head, unwilling to prevent her because he knew why she was striking him. She called to him again when she entered the house.

David came from the kitchen, another boy behind him, both young faces apprehensive.

"Ah, you've got friends!"

"We're cooking supper," he said. "I thought you weren't coming home."

"Am I invited?" She looked past him to his friend, who stood with his thumbs hooked in his pockets, a boy who knew something about her, something told him by David. In his eyes, in his face was his expectation of her as an exciting woman, a woman who had lovers. She was pleased with that expectation, enjoying and deprecating with her own glance his germinal knowledge of her.

"Well, don't we introduce people around here?" She threw her raincoat over a chair in the kitchen, and, learning his name, she shook hands with the boy. He peeled off his sweater, wanting to hide his face from her for the few seconds the sweater went up over his head.

She ate the fried eggs and ham with more gusto than they, sitting indolently sideways at the table so that her crossed legs were around the corner from the boy, almost under his elbow; enjoying his appreciation of her as a woman who complimented him with her nearness, gauche as he was, adolescent as he was. None of the desperation remained from her encounter on the telephone, for in the presence of a stranger her desperation gave way to a charming vivacity. She laughed at the friend's jokes, told in a voice cracked with change and timidity. Then, carried away by her exuberant response to him, he told her a joke that was a joke boys kept among themselves, and she laughed so heartily that she had to hold her head in her hands, elated for that moment by his sight of her as a beautiful, laughing woman who knew boundless more than he did about the joke's meaning.

The friend was the same age as David, fifteen, perhaps a few months older, and with a remarkable symmetry of features. She could, she thought, introduce him to his manhood. She could leave her impression upon him for the rest of his life; she had only to ask him to return. But the boy was not desirable; he was desirable only in a brief fantasy because the fantasy was desirable, animating her body and alleviating the burden of her son's sulking face, that face more beautiful than any face in the world, that face deserted, left out from her involvement with his friend and sensing why it was left out.

She took up her raincoat, slinging it over one shoulder, and, as she went around the table to the door, she trailed her hand across the friend's shoulders and her son's, her touch an endorsement of their friendship that she had not intruded upon but had only fortified—she, the young mother who knew their yearnings more than other women, other mothers.

18

She brought into her home her father's friend, Max Laurie. Years ago he had played the hero's accomplice or confidant, roles that called for an actor of ambiguous looks, either handsome or homely in an attractive, manly way. She remembered him in the movies as having great, dark eyes, a broad face, and a forehead made low by the bangs of black hair; now he was in his fifties, his hair gray, his body smaller. He had been an actor with a name, and he had lost most of his money to three wives and two children. She knew that in his youth he had been virile, that he had basked in women's flirting, and that his grateful surprise with their flirting had endeared him to them. The night she had first met him, years ago during the war—when he had come into the lounge with her father, her father's mistress, and the actress in furs, the night of the day Roosevelt had died—she had been attracted to him. And after he moved up to San Francisco, she had been attracted again whenever she had

met him in the company of her father or of some di-
vorced socialite.

One afternoon she encountered him in a restaurant where she had gone for coffee and cake after
shopping. He told her that he suffered from a heart
condition, gazing at her with an appealing, sorrowing
gleam of doubt, as if no woman could love him because his heart was impaired. Everything he did now
was hesitant—shyness and hesitancy had become part
of the act of the aging celebrity. Years ago he had pretended to be surprised by adoration; now he was truly
surprised by deterioration. It was cancer he was dying
of. Her father, who was his physician, had told her.

He lived in a small apartment, riding a slow, clank-
ing elevator to get up to it and going along a narrow,
dark hallway with mustard-brown walls flecked with
gilt. Outside, the building was very white in the sun.
It rose to twelve floors, way above the others around
it, and had its own parking lot; the interior was a dark
hive. His bed opened out from the wall; the curtains
were heavy and floral, and so was the upholstered fur-
niture. Slick photographs of himself in his most famous
roles were pinned to the walls of the small kitchen.

The love she made to him in the dark apartment
was tender and asked for nothing in return. Lying
against him, caressing his grateful body, she invited
him to come and live with her. He opened alarmed
eyes: "Not an old man with a heart condition." She
kissed the gray, crinkled hairs in the shape of a trian-
gle on his belly and told him that she knew his trouble,

that he had no reason to hide it from her, and that she would take care of him.

She knew that he saw her as her father saw her—uncritically, aware of her faults but amused by them, and amused by her virtues, as if she were still a child forming and growing, and it was not known how she would turn out; but she knew that he was wondering about her reason for wanting to take care of him. At no other time, with no one else, had she demonstrated self-sacrifice. Since he had always carried on a detached flirtation with her, one that an actor would feel called upon to engage in with the daughter of his best friend, she was able to convince him that she had always been drawn to him and that she was making up now for the years she had denied them the rich possibilities of an affair. When he protested that the presence in her home of a man to whom she was not married would be unacceptable to her friends, she mimicked the disapproval he was anticipating on the faces of her friends, and the mimicry roused his actor's admiration for those who put something over harmlessly and with bravura. So he gave up the apartment that he had lived in for seven years and came with his suitcases to her house, and she began to devote herself to him as if it were an involvement she had looked forward to all her life.

She saw to his every comfort, she brought him gifts, cakes of the most lavishly expensive soap, leather brushes, silk pajamas, and at night she went into his room to make love to him. She knew he continued to wonder about her, and that he found no reason for bringing him into her home and giving over her days and nights to serving him. When he was no longer ill at ease, when he no longer accepted her devotion with an edge of toleration as if it were forced upon him, she knew that he no longer wondered.

David had always been entertained by the actor, humored by him, livelier with Max than with anyone else. But now he seemed to have no memory of their friendship. Her son avoided the guest just as he avoided her, but his avoidance of her was more demanding than ever. She felt that his need of her was greater than anyone's need of her, ever, and that her need of him was a somnabulist's need beyond waking caution, and so they passed each other in the house, asking of each other something more than anyone else was able to give. He was rapidly growing tall, and they had a joke about it, the only joke left between them— that he would wake up some morning and raise the roof; and each morning she pretended that he had grown another yard in the night, and she slipped by him, cowering. He was as tall now as his father had been, not heavy in the legs or afflicted with his father's clumsiness, but slender, and there was always a calm alertness in the turn of his head, a grace in the turn of his body.

He was always alone. He brought no friends home, and she sometimes wondered if he had any, but this lack of friends did not trouble her. Instead, she was pleased about it because he seemed in his aloneness to be a more convincing figure of a boy who was to become a man sought after, a man who would make aloneness a way of life and be sought after because of it. His aloneness was proof that he would make something of his life, and she desired this with more fervency than she had ever desired anything for herself; but, passing him and wanting to touch his chest or his face or his dark head to bless him on his way, she held back her hand because she knew it could not bless him.

She devoted herself to Max with the intensity of a penitent. She saw to everything and to that desire which she thought uppermost after his desire to live. She came at night into his room, wearing a negligee or a kimono. She came barefoot down the hall, clean and fragrant from an hour of bathing and massaging herself with lotion; and even during the steep, downhill months, when he often seemed oblivious of her, she continued to come to him.

One night she lay down beside him as usual and opened her clothes in her usual way that was a caressing open. He had lain all afternoon and evening in sedated sleep, moaning and alert to his moaning, waking at the sounds with a start and a look of dread. He took her wrist and thrust her hand away, at the same time turning his face away from hers.

"It's obscene," he complained. "There comes a time when it's obscene."

She was not sure that she had heard him right. He seemed to be muttering in a dream. Wounded, unmoving beside him, she asked him if he was awake.

"God says there's a time and a place for every-thing," he said, his face turned upward again. "I'm awake."

"Let a man die in peace," he said. "Let a man get hold of his mind before he dies. No distractions. I never knew what my mind was for except to make a woman or a buck. Leave me alone so I can get acquainted with my mind. You act like I wait here all day thinking of you. It's obscene when it's not the right time, and the time's not right anymore for me. Last night I dreamed of earth turned over. You know, with a shovel. Or maybe I dreamed it a minute ago. I saw how it looks to God, and I don't like it that way. I'm afraid to see things that way." He sat up to cover himself with the folded blanket at the foot of the bed, unfolding it over himself as he lay down again, unconscious of his act.

She sat up, her back to him, covering her breasts with her negligee. All her life she had been expecting this castigation from men for intruding on their lives, even though they beckoned and begged.

"Viv, listen, little girl," he pleaded. "You have to remember I'm not always in my right mind. Now this way I feel, about the dream, you know, that might mean I'm out of my mind. Maybe I'm not in touch with the mighty things, maybe I'm just dreaming crazy dreams cut down to my size. I don't say no to you because I'm thinking mighty thoughts. Maybe I say no because I'm tired, I don't have the old stuff in me anymore. That's the only reason, there's no big rea-son. You hear me, Viv?"

She said nothing, leaving him to his dream. Someday, some year, somebody was to be left out of her last dream, no matter how much she might love that person, even more than her life.

After that night, she never came again to caress him, and never caressed him while she bathed him and changed his garments unless he caught her hand and laid it upon himself. But in the last months when he could not leave his bed, she was at his call every hour, alleviating—as her father had instructed her—his coughing and his suffering. She lost weight and neglected her appearance. She went around unbathed, her cotton dresses, her linen dresses, bought in anticipation and in enticement of the pleasures of other summers, now soiled and stained. Oblivion was an expression in his eyes; his eyes grew darker each day, more globular, the depths going back to forever, and she felt that she, too, looked that way from gazing so long into his face.

Her father visited Max every other day as the months wore on, concerned more about his daughter's condition of servitude than he was about his friend. His friend was dying, he was not the first or the last to die. When, before, her father had come once a week to play chess with his friend, he had seemed to accept her devotion to the man as something aberrant, inexplicable, and yet something he expected of her and was not surprised by. Now he was surprised at the endurance of her devotion.

One day he sat with her in the patio under the large fringed and scalloped pink umbrella she had bought just before the end of her marriage to Russell, and that now seemed frivolous. For some days her father had tried to convey to her with his deploring eyes his fear that she had lost her mind. She sat under the umbrella with him, her bare legs out in the sun. Every year at the beginning of summer she had always engaged in an indolent race with other women of her circle to acquire an early tan; now, after having denied herself most of the summer sun, it seemed to her that she had not felt the sun's warmth for years. But because her legs were responding to the sun, because she wanted to drop her knees apart, and because her feet in frayed gold mules were warmed, the arches drawing up, she turned her pink canvas chair with great effort toward the table to put herself in the shade again, to deny herself the sun that the man in the house was to be denied forever. With her elbow on the table, she held her chin in her hand, smoking, offering her pale face to her father's deploring eyes, remembering that she was intolerable to him whenever, as a child, her hair was frizzled by a permanent wave or she had grimaced or acted clumsy. On display for him now were her broken fingernails, the spots on her dress, her hair growing in darker, each separate disrepair a separate unhappiness for him because each particular of her beauty had once been so important to her.

"What's going on?" he demanded. "For a while I figured it was some old fixation, some old girlish passion you never let on about, but that's ridiculous. It was ridiculous when I thought of it and more so now as he gets worse. You want to tell me what's going on?"

"He's more comfortable here than at his place," she said.

"That tells me nothing," he said. "The reason he's more comfortable is that you're waiting on him every minute of the day and night. God, I don't know how you stand it. You're not used to anybody dying, like I am, and even I couldn't stand the continual proximity. I avoid dying people. What I want to know is why. You want to tell me why?"

She was silent, her chin in her hand, gazing away from him as if troubled by the sun around her. His mind was pat, she thought, his and her mother's and her brother's, and she waited now for him to produce a pat answer to the question he had asked her. He was, she felt, way up in the top row of the gallery, unable to make sense of her performance, straining for the simple meaning of it.

"It's punishment," he said.

"For what?" she asked him, wondering if he could, in his way, actually come upon an answer.

"It's *like* punishment," he said, more cautious.

"For what?" she repeated.

"You tell me," he said. "You tell me for what."

She cradled her face in both hands, confronting him with her full face like a child waiting for an answer to a riddle. "For my crimes?"

"What the hell crimes have you committed? If it's punishment for a crime, it's one you only imagine you committed."

"I didn't imagine my life," she said, grimacing against the tears, observing his disgust with her grimace and with her fingernails set up to conceal it. "Sometimes I *think* I imagined it."

"Oh, God," he said. "You're nowhere near the menopause and you're wailing about what you did and didn't do with your life." He reached out to grasp her wrist, consolingly.

"You don't like to see my face when it cries," she said, pulling away from his hand. They sat for several minutes in silence.

"Maybe I'm punishing myself because I let too many men see me cry," she said. "I shouldn't have done that to them, or to me. And I don't mean just cry. There are ways of crying other than this way. There are ways like accusations, like belittling, like ways I don't want to say. If you think I'm punishing myself, taking care of Max, you may be right."

Again they were both silent. Then, veering away from the unfamiliar, her father went on. "You ought to make yourself attractive to him. It worries him that you're neglecting yourself. He told me. He feels responsible, of course. Otherwise," he said, having received no promise, no reply, "he'll figure you want everybody to know what you're doing for him. You're making something terribly public about it, looking that way."

"Nobody sees me," she said.

"So nobody comes by anymore?" he asked, derisively.

"Max's wife, his last one," she said. "That's all."

"Your son sees you," he said. "He's more important than the others, anyway. You ever wonder what he thinks—his mother waiting on a stranger day and night, looking like a hag?"

"He'll understand when he's older."

"I'm older and I don't understand."

"You're not David."

She walked beside him around the house to his car, impressing her presence upon him, her ravaged presence, so that if ever he was to have any greater knowledge of her, he would remember that she had atoned for whatever she had done in her life that ought to be atoned for.

19

The presence of Max Laurie was like a great impassable hand between herself and her son. The disintegration of the man, the constant grappling for his body by nothingness, served as a barrier between herself and her son, who was becoming, that summer of his sixteenth year, the man she had imagined for him when he was a child.

Each day of the warm spell at the end of summer she bathed Max's body as he lay in his bed. "I wish I had never hurt anybody in my life," he said to her, stroking her arm.

"How many have you hurt?" she asked, humoringly.

"Everybody I've ever known," he said. "Not deliberately. I'll say deliberately, because in the back of my mind I knew what I was doing. I used to say it was circumstance, but I think it was me. I don't know what it was. It might have been circumstance after all. But whatever it was, nobody should be hurt. They'll die too, and whatever dies shouldn't be hurt while it's alive."

"You want to be a saint?" she asked.

He frowned a deep, intolerant frown that closed his eyes, a frown that was a revelation to her of the turbulence at his core. Then, still with his eyes closed, he began stroking her arm again.

"The only reason I'm talking this way," he said, "is because I'm sorry nobody knows who the other one is, what's troubling him, what's in his heart. I don't know why you brought me here. I know it wasn't because of any great love for me. I don't know why, but you've been more than kind, and whatever it is that's troubling you, I want you to know that I wish I could help you, and that's the way I want you to remember me—that I wished I could help you."

"You help me," she assured him.

"Sometimes I feel like I haven't been tested yet," he went on, "that my life hasn't been lived yet. I feel like a boy who hasn't been put to the test yet, and I feel old, like I've been through the mill. I feel both. But I think I feel mostly that I haven't been tested yet, that more was expected of me. But what? What more? I should have done what I want others to do for me now—weep over me. It's the indifference that scares me. When so many die at once, in the war, in the concentration camps, what else can you do but be indifferent when one man passes out of the picture? Or maybe it was the indifference that led to everything. That's why I feel my life hasn't been lived yet. What did I do about the indifference? Was I supposed to do something about it?"

"I don't know, I don't know." The cloth was absorbing the heat of his body. She dipped it into the bowl of tepid water and continued to bathe him, resisting the loss he was leading her into, the loss not only of him but of all the men of her life, the men she had believed were all more than this man's body was telling her they were.

He stroked her bare arm, down from the shoulder. "I wish somebody would keep a light on for me, like my mother did for my father," he said. "It's one of those Jewish customs I forgot about. You light a candle or you keep an electric light on—every year on the day the person died. For his spirit. We had a dark hall in the apartment, we left the light on there. The way mother told it to me, it's to light his way to God. I used to think it took an awfully long time for him to find his way, it went on year after year. It's just a matter of being remembered, that's all. I did it one year for my mother and then I forgot, or I was ashamed to do it. Depends on who you're living with at the time. Maybe nobody does it anymore. Not since so many died at once. What's one light? But I think I'd like you to do it for me anyway. No promises, nothing like that," he insisted. "No promises."

20

When Max was taken to the hospital she kissed his brow and his hands in the presence of her father. She promised him, kissing his hands, that she would come by to visit him the next morning. Although he appeared to know what was happening to him, that he was being conveyed away, he did not seem aware of her kissing or of her promise or even of her presence.

In the hour following, she sat out in the garden, grieving over him, knowing that she would not visit him tomorrow or any day, that the sight of him while she kissed him had been the last sight. Around her she heard the sounds of the neighborhood's tranquility on a warm evening at the end of summer, but listened for sounds of violence and for violence without sound and for the return of her son that would deafen her to all sounds. With cigarettes falling from the package held upside down in her hands, she wandered into the living room and lay down on the sofa to wait for him. Exhausted by the heat of the day and by the countless nights of interrupted sleep, she slept, and was wakened by the fear that her son was not returning. It was night. She lit the lamp by the sofa and slept again.

"Is Max dead?"

She found she was lying on her side with her hands under her cheek, like a child. He had asked if Max was dead, she knew, because she had thrown herself on the sofa and appeared to be waiting to tell him. For no other reason would she be lying out there so startlingly.

"Where were you?" she demanded, sitting up, her question accusing him of solitude, of his young and slender body, of his response to the night, his skin paled by the night but everything else deepened—his curiosity, his innocence, his eyes. "You don't know and you don't care, that's what you think of Max." He went on toward the stairs to escape her anger, and she called after him, "David? Do you hear me?"

She followed him to where he waited by the stairs, his back to the wall. "They took him away," she cried, gripping his arms, lifting her face for him to see the spasms of grief, and he put his hand clumsily at the back of her head and pressed her face against his chest. With her hands covering her face, she went with him up the stairs as though returning to her bed to find rest and a cessation of grief and of all demands upon her, glimpsing through her fingers her bare feet climbing.

They sat together on her bed in an embrace of grief, until his consoling, his stroking her face and hands drew her down, drew him down beside her. She held his head with both her hands so that he could not elude her mouth moving over his face as if they both would die if she lifted it away, as if she were charged with the task of keeping them both alive. Against her mouth she felt his face pleading with her to save him from the world's chaos and to take him into the heart of that chaos. She undressed him and herself, his clothes among her own, as if she undressed one body, freeing them both from the flickering show of concealing and revealing that had gone on for the years of his life, and at last he lay beside her as he was to lie beside other women who were to be less now, forever less, than she, even as everyone in his life to come was to be less. She took his hands, guiding them to console her over more sorrow than he could ever imagine, guiding his body onto her body, at last obliterating the holy separateness she had given him at birth.

Stricken by the same fear, then, they were unable to move apart. The fear that someone, everyone, would discover them if they moved, that even the slightest movement would reveal them, that everyone in their life must sense their presence here together and would sound the alarm if they attempted to return into the order of things. Furtively, in stages, she unbent her legs, but he moved suddenly, arresting his body in a nightmare fall, and she held him down, warningly. The lamp by the bed was on; holding him to her with one arm, she lifted her other arm to switch it off. Then, in the dark, it seemed to her that she had never been so conscious. Never so conscious before of her dominion.

21

The hour before dawn foretold how stifling the day was to be. Although his face was only a few inches away, it seemed to have suddenly receded far into the past, lapsing into sleep, into unconsciousness to elude a comprehension as hoveringly near as her face. She drew herself away from him. She found her negligee on the floor and, drawing it around her, wondered where to go to hide from him so that when he woke he could claim he woke from a dream. But when she moved toward the door, he flung himself off the bed, falling to the floor.

The sounds of his body thrashing against the floor deafened her to her own voice calling to him. Kneeling by him, she found him very still, the stillness as frightening as his paroxysm.

"I'll sleep here, I'll sleep here," he said. But when she stood up, relieved to hear him speak of sleep, he lifted his head, coiling himself toward her feet, biting her ankle above the place his hands gripped it.

She struggled to be free, wailing, and he released her, flinging himself away from her.

She went out to the garden and lay down on the canvas cot, on the scattered leaves. She lay unmoving in the warm dark that was filled with the voices of birds like the sound of daylight breaking through in many small places, and, sleeping, dreamed that she was running backward into sleep, a stumbling, ungainly, heavy backward run into sleep, escaping her son running toward her, her son at the age of three or four, in a white suit, with everything clean upon him, running toward her to wipe his face in her skirt and leave an irremovable stain.

She opened her eyes to the sunlight of midmorning and closed them again. She was lying in the sun, unprotected by shadow, exhausted by the sun and by sleep itself, by the days and nights without sleep, by the memory of the night, and unable to rise and drag the cot into shade. She slept again, this time her sleep an oppression upon her like a sorrowfully familiar body, and woke to the sun exactly overhead, her face upward to it, the negligee fallen open and her body in a slattern's torpor. Rising, she returned to the house through the dense, obscuring sun, but stood outside the door, afraid to enter and afraid to see him again, wanting never to see him again and never to be seen by him, and, at the same time, feeling the loss of him as if he had died while she slept and her grief was never to be less.

For the rest of the day she remained in the garden,

by the table in the shade of the umbrella, or wandering the narrow flagstone paths, waiting for her son to come out to her and forgive her. At the end of the afternoon, overcome by the conviction that she had denied all day, the conviction that he was gone, she entered the house. The silence, and even the fact that she could not find him, did not prove that he was gone; the silence was his taciturnity that she had experienced for so long. She accepted his absence only when she stood by the window of her bedroom, looking down on the leaf-littered cot where she had lain. Sometime during the morning, she knew, he had looked down, and it was to be his last sight of her.

22

Early in the evening she went out, afraid that he might
return that night. She concealed her face with cosmet-
ics like an actress hoping to conceal herself with a false
face. She put on a yellow taffeta dress she had bought
a year ago when Max had come to live with her; she
put on her gray calf shoes whose color was a subtle silver, also bought a year ago; and though the night was
warm she put on her long mink coat that Russell had
given her for her birthday, their last year together. She
had the appearance of a woman convalescing, who, in
haste, in terror of falling ill again, applies her beauty
awry. Afraid to remain at home and afraid to go out,
she drove to her parents' house. The excuse that she
gave to her mother, who was home alone, was that she
had been on her way to a dinner party and felt ill and,
since she had been near to her mother's house, she had
decided to rest there awhile.

"My God, Viv, furs. It's a warm night," her mother
said when Vivian threw off her coat to lie down on

the sofa. "Is it chills and fever?" She placed her small, smooth palm on Vivian's forehead. "You're tired out. You've exhausted yourself taking care of Max. Are you cold?" She laid the fur coat over her daughter, up and over the breasts in the tight, saffron taffeta cups and up over the bare shoulders. "You may have caught something from him. I don't mean what he had, of course. I mean something else—the fear. When a young person like you is around somebody who's dying, she can't help but catch the fear."

"It's something I drank," Vivian called after her mother, who was already on her way through the delicately tinted rooms to the kitchen. She lay waiting for whatever her mother would bring, gazing down the length of her body, the length of the fur coat, to her feet in the silver shoes. If any confession was ever to be made it would not be made to her mother. A confession could never be made to any woman; there was more shame in confessing to a woman and nothing to be gained by it, no forgiveness that meant anything. To confess to a man, whether it led him to despise her or to forgive her, meant more, but it was not to be made to any man, either. She drew the coat over her mouth and nose.

Her mother returned, bearing a teapot and cups on a tray. "If you'd rather have coffee or sherry . . ."

"No, no, it's tea I wanted." She swung her legs down and sat up, holding her coat up around her to her chin, and reaching around it to lift the cup and saucer from the tray.

"You're thin," her mother said. "You're thin as a rail. You ought to go to Hawaii. Teresa's there—she's always lots of fun—and some of your friends." She found her niece's letter in a novel on the coffee table, unfolded it, and read, while Vivian held the coat to her chin and sipped tea, commenting on the pleasures to be found in the islands.

"You haven't been out in so long," her mother said, apparently wondering if the year of her daughter's devotion to Max had damaged her wits so that, the day after the man was taken away, she stumbled out into the world, dressed as though on her way to a ball and going nowhere. "You look beautiful, but you've got so thin and you don't look after yourself. You ought to have gone to Nicole's to have your hair done."

The china began to rattle in Vivian's hands, and, leaning forward, she set the cup and saucer on the rug by her feet. "David ran away," she said, her head down, her fingers unable to release the rattling china.

"Vivian, lie down," her mother begged.

She lay down again and her mother drew the coat over her again.

"Where did he go?"

"At this point I don't care where he went. At this point he's on his own. At this point I don't care if he never shows up again. I never told you, did I, how jealous he was?" She threw off the coat and sat up. "What time is it?"

"Do you want me to phone and tell them you're not coming?" her mother asked.

"No, because I'm going," she said. She got into her coat with her mother's help. "You can't imagine how jealous he was of Max. Can you imagine—of Max? Not just him," she cried. "Of everybody. Of Russell. Because I don't come and tell you my troubles, you think I've got none."

"I know about them," her mother said.

"He's gone to the Pastori family at Clearlake. That's where he wanted to go. They've got a boy his age. He'll be all right. I drove him to the bus depot," she said, wanting to dispel the alarm from her mother's face, wanting no face near her that showed alarm.

She went upstairs with her mother because no one was waiting for her to sit down with the rest of the party. Her old room was immaculate, satin shining on the bed and walnut glowing. The silver-framed photograph of herself at the age of twelve in a ballet pose was obscured by the reflected light on the glass that covered it. She undressed while her mother was out of the room finding a nightgown for her, and, waiting, she covered herself with her slip, afraid that her mother would sense, at the sight of her nakedness, what use the daughter had made of her body. She let the slip fall to her lap as her mother helped her draw on the gown, a pink gown fragrant with sachets, yielding to the gown like a small girl who needs help with undressing.

"I told him to go," she said. "'Goddamn it, go,' I said. 'What do you think, that you're going to stay with me forever, looking at me with those baleful eyes?' Isn't that what kind of eyes he has? Like some-body in a storybook? Animals and awful creatures? Mama, you remember?"

Sitting up in bed, she held up the palm of her hand submissively for the capsule her mother put there, swallowing it down with port wine from the decanter that was kept in her mother's room.

23

She waited for him with dread, and the few times she went out she expected to find him somewhere in the house when she returned. Waking in the morning or at noon or in the night, she was at once alert to the possibility of his presence by her bed. Wanting to be far away, she was unable to leave because he had no other person to return to; there was no other person from whom he had got sustenance, got love.

In the second week of his absence, a letter came from Las Vegas, from Paul, his father. Through the years, he had sent the boy a few letters and a snapshot of himself and his wife, smiling into the glaring sun of that desert city. David was with them, he wrote, and although the boy had asked them not to tell her, they were sure she was troubled by his disappearance and they thought it best to inform her of his whereabouts. And for another reason it was best: the boy was miserable, and they were trying to persuade him to return to her so that she and David could talk over their bad feelings and forgive each other for whatever the quarrel was about. A few days after the first letter a second came: David had been put aboard a bus to San Francisco. She waited with the curtains closed. On the sixth day, when she went out to the sidewalk box to pick up the accumulation of mail, she found a letter from David, mailed from Galveston, Texas. The sight of his handwriting was like a confrontation. She could not stand, and sat down on the steps to read.

Vivian. In large letters, with pencil, her name was scrawled across the top of the scrap of paper. *I want you to die. If you die I won't have to. I hope when you read this it will be like a curse that works. Maybe you won't even get to this line.* He had not signed his name.

She left the city that day, driving her mother, and her mother's two poodles, to her parents' summer home on the shore of Lake Tahoe. She lay out in the sun on the wide deck of the house, drowsing and pretending to drowse, wakened often by the fear that he was gazing down at her from upstairs, sometimes shaken awake by her mother, who said that she had been crying in her sleep. In her mother's face she saw how her own face must appear down on the cushions. Her mother's face, bending over hers, was her own face in the years to come, the face of herself as a past woman, alone and alarmed; and she drew her mother down upon her.

At her mother's urgings she had her hair cut and bleached again, and she had a manicure and a pedicure.

She bought flamboyantly flowered, very slim dresses from the resort shops, and delicate sandals with high heels and no backs, and, urged by her mother to a display of this artful care of her person, she strolled out with the two poodles into the crowds. Although she despised them for their yapping and the tension of their bodies, she reluctantly enjoyed the spectacle of herself and the dogs, whose fur was the white of her hair, all three of them exquisitely groomed.

After her mother's return to the city with the dogs, Vivian stayed on, spending her afternoons in the cool bars and in the casinos, bringing home her small winnings and sometimes a man she had chosen to sit down by. A long time ago, her first love after the birth of her son had separated her body from the infant's, but now the men she brought to her bed to obliterate her son failed to convince her that the body she lay against was not her son's, and waking with someone beside her was always a time of panic.

On her return to the city, late in October, she sold the house with its furnishings and antiques, taking with her only enough for her small apartment on Green Street in a building of four apartments signed over to her by her father shortly after the war. With her mother she sailed to Hawaii. On the boat, her mother, excited by the voyage, imagined that everyone mistook them for sisters, that her twenty-five years beyond her daughter's age were swept away by the sea winds. They stayed at one of the more seclusive hotels where they could settle down for a time without the constant bustling change of other guests and, in March, returned home by air.

She took a separate taxi, declining to go home to her mother's house. In the apartment, she sat down on the sofa, clasping herself, shivering with the change of climate as if the transition from sun to fog had taken no more than a minute. When the sound of the cab driver's footsteps, running down the stairs, was gone, the silence in the apartment, whose location and existence her son was ignorant of, became the silence that had swallowed both herself and her son.

Not long after her return, Joe Duggan, the attorney who had often visited in the time of her marriage to Russell, asked her out to dinner. He had separated from his wife; she had learned this some time ago. She disliked the man; he had always insinuated a knowledge of her and it had seemed to her that the basis for any insinuation was ignorance. She felt that he conversed not with her but with the woman he thought she was, while she sat listening to the dialogue like a third person. But, as in other times when she had been in need of someone, her criticism of her companion began to seem flimsy, and she wanted to believe he was capable of that knowledge of her most personal self. Then everything became attractive—his indisputable voice, his obviously elegant clothes, and his little blond mustache that was like a stamp of approval on his face.

In his apartment, with its leased view of the bay and the bridges, he inquired after David, and she told him what she had told her parents, that the boy was attending a private school in the East. He recalled the night at Clearlake when David had danced with all the women, also recalling that she had gone upstairs before the others. Insinuative, self-amused, he lay beside her, recalling.

"You've got everything, Viv," he said, "but one thing."

"What?" she asked, afraid.

"Something you had with Russell."

"What? What?"

"Something I couldn't have then. Now that you're with me, you don't have it anymore. All it is is what I couldn't have then." He held in his laughter; she felt the sputter against her throat. "Otherwise, you've got everything."

She could not bring herself to push him away. He knew so very little that his ignorance of her was like an unbearable vulgarity. And yet, with his lewd curiosity, he seemed to know everything, if only because he suspected everything. Lying beside him, she found that the memory of her son, the night with her son, was being reduced to what it would be in Duggan's mind if he knew about it, even as her life was being reduced to what it was in his mind. His curiosity forgave everything because everything fed his curiosity. Unresisting, she lay under him, kissing him in return, accepting his ignorance of her as if it were a forgiving wisdom.

In July, a few days before David's birthday, a letter

came from him, postmarked El Centro, California, and forwarded from the house she had left. The handwriting was a barrier between him and herself, a fence beyond which all his experiences in the past year had gone on. It was written in ink, the letters neater and smaller than in the first letter. He was working, he wrote, on a date farm near the Mexican border. On his seventeenth birthday he wanted to enlist in the army, and that was why he was writing to her—because he required her consent.

She was unable, for a few days, to answer the letter or to go a notary to make out her consent. The request from her son surrounded her with the terrors of the world, as if only now she had been born into the midst of them. One night she dreamed that he was dying. He lay on her bed, in an army uniform, his head shaven. He begged her to lift him and carry him away in her arms to some place safe from death, but she was unable to approach him. She had entered the room with a group of strangers behind her, who appeared to be waiting for her to save him, but she could do nothing. The sensation of dying was in herself as it was in him.

She sought out a notary and found one in a hotel, in a cubicle off the lobby, a gray-haired woman whose eyes seemed a part of her bejeweled spectacles. In the legalistic words suggested by the notary, she gave her consent for her son to enter the army, and, after the consent was typed and she had signed it, she asked for an envelope. Then, pushing pennies across the corner of the desk with the tip of a gloved finger, she asked apologetically to buy a stamp.

Early in September, Duggan flew to Washington in the interests of a case, and from there to New York. The first few nights he telephoned her. On the fifth night he failed to call and she lay awake, reading, knowing it was too late for him to phone, but expecting him to wake up in the middle of the night on the other side of the country and remember that he had not phoned her, and in his imagination see her waiting. She fell asleep, waking at one o'clock to the light of the lamp she had left on, and, in that moment of surprising light, she was reminded of Max and of his plea to her to leave a light burning for him. She could not recall the date that he had died because she had never known the date. It was a short time after he was taken away; she had been told the day, but she had not known the date of that day and she had not attended his funeral. One night was as good as another as long as a year had gone by. He would, she felt, forgive her if she were in error by a few days.

With the light full on her face, she lay against the several pillows she had propped herself with to read, glad that there was no one around to ridicule her about the ritual or to disapprove of it, no one around to feel like an outsider in what might appear to be a most personal engagement of hers with someone not there. The light in the room seemed remote from its purpose. It was simply a light in an apartment among hundreds of lights in apartments all over the city, and how was one light to be separated from all others as the one that remembered him and lit his way? The purpose of the light was remote from the light, even as the ritual was remote from her, even as the man himself had been remote, even as all of them were remote. There was no illumination of anybody other than herself, lying alone, waiting for one of the remote ones to return and lie down beside her.

GINA BERRIAULT was an American novel-
ist and short story writer. Throughout her life,
she published four novels and three short story
collections, including the collection *Women
in Their Beds*, which won a PEN/Faulkner
Award for Fiction and a National Book Critics
Circle Award. A grant recipient from the National Endowment for the Arts, Berriault was
also a Guggenheim Fellow, the recipient of a
Rea Award for the Short Story, a Gold Medal
from the Commonwealth Club of California,
a Pushcart Prize, and several O'Henry prizes.
She died in 1999.